A Glimpse *of* Mercy

Trophies of Grace Series
BOOK 3

Betty J Hassler

WESTBOW
PRESS®
A DIVISION OF THOMAS NELSON
& ZONDERVAN

WestBow Press books may be ordered through booksellers or by contacting:

WestBow Press
A Division of Thomas Nelson & Zondervan
1663 Liberty Drive
Bloomington, IN 47403
www.westbowpress.com
844-714-3454

Unless otherwise cited, scriptures are taken from the HOLY BIBLE: NEW INTERNATIONAL VERSION®.© 1973, 1978, 1984 by International Bible Society. Used by permission of Zondervan. All rights reserved.

Scripture quotations marked (NLT) are taken from the Holy Bible, New Living Translation, copyright © 1996. Used by permission of Tyndale House Publishers, Inc., Wheaton, Illinois 60189. All rights reserved.

ISBN: 979-8-3850-0339-6 (sc)
ISBN: 979-8-3850-0340-2 (e)

Library of Congress Control Number: 2023913647

Print information available on the last page.

WestBow Press rev. date: 08/22/2023

To those who have shown mercy to me
and to whom I've had the divine privilege
of showing mercy

But if you have been merciful, God will be merciful.
James 2:13 NLT

A NOTE FROM THE AUTHOR

Have you ever experienced mercy? Perhaps a policeman let you off with a warning ticket. A neighbor waved off the offense when you ran over her flower bed. Your lab puppy didn't snarl when you accidentally stepped on his paw.

God's mercy is infinitely greater than what we can offer to each other. His mercy requires more than forgiving or not holding a grudge. Because of His holiness, He can't tolerate sin. Someone has to pay the price. God chose a lamb without blemish, a sinless man who was a worthy sacrifice, to die in our place. That is the ultimate offer of mercy. None of us wants justice because we are guilty as charged. In turn for His mercy, our Father asks us to put aside the justice we think we deserve in order to follow the example of our Master. Mercy is an act of humility, trusting God to be the judge.

In *A Glimpse of Mercy,* the main characters demonstrate how costly it is to give mercy to others, and, in kind, to receive mercy from them. For each one the experience is a process.

Book 3 stands alone (as do the others in the Trophies of Grace series). You'll soon catch on to the relationships between the characters. However, if you'd like a guide to this third generation of the Brooks-Hamilton families, turn to pages 166-167 for a family tree. These fictional characters live in Nashville, Tennessee, where I made my home for eighteen years.

I thank God for giving me the vision for this series. It pray it will demonstrate through the lives of everyday people how He lavishes His children with *A Beam of Hope, A Stash of Faith,* and now *A Glimpse of Mercy.* May it remind us all that God's mercy is to be returned in kind to those around us.

PROLOGUE

December, 2018

Layton Brooks carefully opened the doors of his trophy case, which rested against the back wall of his man cave. Dust cloth in hand, he held the first trophy up to the sunlight and began to dust. Each trophy had been engraved with a person's name, date, and character trait he or she represented. He'd presented the trophies to each person, calling them his heroes of faith. These spiritual mentors had demonstrated a quality that he wanted to emulate.

Layton would tell those who witnessed the trophy presentations that they had gathered "to build faith muscles," as he put it. Now, as he took each trophy in his hands, memories flowed, along with a few tears.

Trophy 1 to Amy Brooks, his dear wife, for *forgiveness*
Trophy 2 to Brianne Brooks, his only child, for *endurance*
Trophy 3 to Myra Norwell, his pastor's wife, for *peace*
Trophy 4 to his mother-in-law, Jan Dyer, for the gift of *hope*
Trophy 5 to Abigail Sloan in absentia for demonstrating *faith*
Trophy 6 to Parker Sloan Hamilton for the *freedom* award

As he dusted the emptied shelves, he recalled how the trophy case got its name. The idea came from his mother-in-law. Brianne had just survived cancer for the first time. Her Meme Dyer was saying goodbye at the Nashville airport. Meme declared that God's good purposes in Brianne's illness would be a trophy of His grace.

Meme's optimism had been the inspiration for a trophy case to display God's grace. *Grace is God's way of treating us as though we are deserving of His blessings—although, of course, we're not.* As Layton replaced each trophy on the shelves, he wondered who would be the next person God would lead him to acknowledge in this simple way. He closed the doors and busied himself with the rest of the furniture in his man cave.

"Good job there." Layton turned to see his wife Amy in the doorway. "You're getting an early start on preparing for our Christmas guests."

"Holly will be home in a few days, and life tends to get a little hectic when she's around. I figured I'd better get a head start." He ambled to the couch and patted the seat beside him. Amy sat down, a quizzical look on her lovely face. Layton responded, "I just thought we'd take a moment to rest. Holly is a wallflower compared to our surprise guests who'll be here soon."

"Point." Amy rested her reddish curls on his shoulder. The few streaks of gray he saw woven through her locks simply added illumination to the darkening room. Layton's mind kept spinning despite his comfortable position. What was it Meme Dyer always said? *God's up to something in this family. You just wait and see.*

Holly Brianne Hamilton rested her chin on her younger brother's strawberry-blonde head. Standing behind the sofa where he sat, she had a direct view of the Internet site on his iPhone. She reached past his shoulder and clicked on a pop-up menu.

"Hey, knock it off." Ty pushed her arm away.

"How'd you know it was me?" she asked in wide-eyed innocence.

"I wonder," he groused. Holly tousled his strawberry curls before settling into an armchair nearby. Tyler, or Ty as the family called him, seemed to have grown taller while she was away at Georgetown University for her first semester. With his mother's hair color and ocean-blue eyes, plus his dad's height and build, he combined the best features of both parents. She had to admit Ty was *hot*—at least to girls who weren't his sister.

Holly couldn't believe he'd completed half his senior year of high school, and she'd barely heard a word about it. "Ty, don't you have any Christmas shopping left? Let's go somewhere."

He glared at her. "Not on your life."

She started to ask why. Then she remembered their most recent outing. Outside the food court at the mall, a girl who liked Ty smiled in his direction. Holly took his arm possessively and steered him inside a nearby store. Ty jerked free, but the damage was done.

Was it her fault the girl hadn't guessed they were brother and sister? With her father's dark hair and eyes and her mom's petite form, Holly didn't resemble her brother. In more ways than physical, they were opposites. *Strange,* she thought. *Same gene pool.*

Apparently, Ty hadn't appreciated her prank. Nor was it forgiven or forgotten. Now, when she wanted to hang out, her prank had cost her his company.

Ty's phone rang. Quickly, he clicked to answer. "Yeah ... Sure ... Sounds good."

"Who was that?" Always curious, Holly tried to get a look at the name.

"None of your business."

Holly took the rebuff in stride. Ty was a quiet, shy kid, who seemed to manage life with little interference from his parents or sister. His pensive moods often left her wondering what was going on in his thick head. On the other hand, she was a babbling brook, who daily regaled her family with elaborate accounts of her adventures.

Surely, I can break through that shell of his, she mused. She folded her arms resolutely. The Christmas holidays would be a good time to try and make a dent.

Meanwhile, her mind turned to more immediate concerns. Taking out her cell phone, Holly glanced at the time. "Has the mail come?" she asked in a loud voice to no one in particular.

Her mom peered around the corner from the kitchen. "Why do you want to know?"

Bounding to her side, Holly gave her an agonized look. "For eighteen years I've suffered the cruel fate of a Christmas Eve birth. On the positive side, my nineteenth birthday is days away." She closed her eyes and dramatically held out her open palms to her mother. "Please hand over my deluge of packages, money, and gift cards."

Brianne Brooks Hamilton steered her daughter toward the kitchen island to survey her treasure trove, which she had carefully sorted into stacks. Holly fingered the cards, eyes still closed. The biggest one, no doubt from Holly's grandmother, Olivia Sloan Hamilton, would include a large, impersonal check. Her son Gavin, Holly's dad, had already explained that his mother would be spending Christmas in Italy with his sister, Alexis.

Holly could count on one hand the times she had seen her Aunt Alexis in person. She was a little-known fashion designer whose long-term relationship with a wealthy Italian live-in had produced no marriage or children. Alexis would probably send her the usual gift card packaged with a scenic picture of her draped across some gorgeous Italian landmark.

Holly opened her eyes and looked through the other cards, mostly from family friends. The lone package was from Kyle Brooks, Grandpa Brooks's brother, who always sent something related to his years in the diplomatic corps. Exotic treasures, usually jewelry or cultural knickknacks, awaited her. Eagerly, she picked up the package.

Holly had the ability to take a present, shake and wiggle it, weigh it in her hands, smell it, listen intently, and often guess its contents. This talent lent a certain mystique to her reputation as an amateur sleuth.

"Simple curiosity will take you amazing places," she'd tell her friends. Ty called her a snoop, and her dad complained about her penchant for finding his chocolate hiding places. As Holly stood lost in thought, her mom snatched the cards and gift away and began to hide them in a cupboard. "You know not to open anything for two more days."

"Okay. At least I know they're in a safe *findable* place." Holly ducked before her mom swatted her with a kitchen towel. Her mom's laugh quickly turned into a nasty coughing fit. Holly grabbed a glass and filled it with water. Handing it to her, she studied her mom's slender frame. "That cough is awful. Shouldn't you take something for it?"

When the coughing subsided, her mom downplayed the incident. "I am. I had that respiratory infection right after Thanksgiving. Then, a week ago I caught a cold. My cough is the last mutinous villain to kill." She gave Holly a wicked grin.

Holly wasn't convinced. As she headed back to the family room, she said a silent prayer for her mom, who had a busy few days ahead. Family gatherings at Christmas were noisy, active affairs in the Hamilton/Brooks households with plenty of food and festivities. The birthday girl frowned, wondering if her mom could handle it all.

Gavin Hollister Hamilton walked into the house from the garage, through the mud room, and down the hallway to his study. He passed Holly's and Ty's rooms, noting neither was there. In his home office, he threw his jacket on an armchair and deposited his briefcase next to the desk. Enticing smells from the kitchen drew him back the way he'd come and right into the arms of his lovely wife.

"Aw, I thought I had sneaked in." He planted a kiss on Brianne's cheek.

She grinned. "You did, but I was lying in wait. Somehow, I just knew you'd head for the kitchen."

Gavin held her close. The two rocked silently back and forth. He might be a force to contend with in a courtroom, but his wife could sway him like a reed. Brianne had captured his heart at a time in his life when no one of her caliber should have cared about him, much less grown to love him.

"How did I get so lucky to be standing here hugging you?"

Brianne loosened his tie in a playful gesture. "Well … you had a mentor named Layton Brooks, who just happened to have a lovely daughter—that would be me. Besides, I worked for your brother Parker at The Sloan House. A happy coincidence, don't you think?"

"Yeah. A chance meeting." He laughed. "The rest, as they say, is history."

Brianne rested her head on his shoulder. Gavin wondered for the millionth time how she could have fallen in love with a former alcoholic and drug user. He'd gotten clean largely through the efforts and prayers of his older brother, Parker, who had saved his life after an overdose.

Reluctantly, Gavin released his bride of twenty years. "Thanks again for loving me."

"It's a tough job, but — somebody's got to do it." They finished the sentence together.

Brianne drew her pretty face into a scowl. "You know I don't like you working on a Saturday."

"I'm taking all of next week off. Christmas break, you know." He headed in the direction of the wondrous smells emanating from the stove. "Had to clear up some last-minute things. How're the kids?"

"Holly is obsessed with her birthday and Ty—well, he's just Ty. They're around here somewhere."

He opened the oven door, lifted the lids off pans cooking on the stove, and got his hand swipped with Brianne's kitchen towel. The usual.

Later that evening, Holly made hot chocolate and set steaming mugs around the kitchen table. Enticed by the smell and Holly's invitation, the other family members took their customary seats. In her usual take charge way, she asked, "So what's been going on with everybody lately?

Gavin glanced at Brianne, who'd once been known as the take-charge queen. Brianne raised her arms in a sign of surrender. "Like mother, like daughter."

Unfazed by the comparison, Holly continued. "I'll start."

With a knowing smile, her mom begged, "Oh, tell us about it. Please."

Holly ignored her mom's teasing and launched into her account. "I'm going to hunt for a seasonal job. I have a whole month between semesters at Georgetown. I really want to make some extra money. You'd think Nordstrom would hire me. I practically lived there during high school."

"I remember." Her dad patted his wallet.

Holly turned to him. "Perhaps I'll just lie around the house instead and rest up—after all that trouble I went to spending your money in DC." He gave her a playful poke in the ribs. "So, Dad, tell us about one of your latest wheelin' dealin' legal shenanigans."

"Thanks for your vote of confidence in my integrity, honey." He winked and crossed his arms behind his head. "You'll enjoy this story. A potential client shows up at my law office. Seems he owns land near a bridge used by the Nashville homeless as a gathering spot. He wants the city to consider him a non-profit housing agency and reduce his taxes."

After the chuckles subsided, Holly's mom shared a conversation she'd had with her mother, Amy Brooks. Despite her semi-retirement from interior design, Nana—as the grandchildren called her—still worked as a home stylist for several local realtors. "Nana tried to talk an elderly couple into putting away the 32 family pictures hanging in the main entry of their home. She told them buyers want a house to feel like a place they can see themselves living in—not a monument to the present owners. The couple refused. They want to keep the entry 'as is.'"

Holly groaned. "So, Mom, anything new with The Sloan Foundation?"

Having grown up playing in her mom's home office, she knew the ends and outs of working for a non-profit.

Her uncle, Parker Hamilton, had started the foundation for those just released from prison on probation or recovering addicts. His own stay in a halfway house had cemented his new faith in Christ. After opening The Sloan House in Nashville, Parker had begun numerous halfway houses around the country. In addition, his foundation lobbied for prison reform and addiction funding at state capitals and in Washington, DC. Holly volunteered in the DC office when her studies at Georgetown University allowed.

Her mom lifted her cup of chocolate and paused. "Actually, I haven't been working as much lately. Since competing for public funding for the foundation has grown harder in recent years, Uncle Parker has to rely more on cultivating wealthy donors. That means more traveling and speaking events. I see him less and less. But he and Aunt Kathy are hosting the family Christmas Day."

Holly thought about the implications of her mom's announcement. How could The Sloan Foundation get by with fewer hours from its administrative assistant and chief grant writer? She'd have to quiz her mom later to get more details.

Throughout the conversation, Holly had kept an eye on Ty, who sat quietly, turning his empty mug back and forth in his hands. "Harrumph." Holly cleared her throat. "Ty, when you get through playing with your mug, would you care to report on your day?"

He locked eyes with her. "Well, my sister has been home one day, and she's already getting on my nerves. That's about it. Same old, same old. Glad to be out of school on break." Ty picked up his mug and leisurely headed for the kitchen sink. Holly watched as her mom and dad exchanged glances.

She thought quickly. "Hey, bro, I'll liven things up by beating you at any video game you choose. Your place or mine?"

"Neutral territory," Ty countered and headed toward the family room.

"You're on." Holly followed him. Somehow. Someway. She'd get beneath the surface of Ty's exterior. If he had anything going on that should be a concern, big sis would be on the case in a nanosecond. She might be a snoop, but in this case, she trusted that her inquisitive nature would serve her brother well.

Ty was the package she had yet to open—the one that eluded her detective skills. The one whose contents she had yet to guess.

Propped up on two pillows, Gavin lay in bed and pretended to read a legal brief while Brianne prepared for bed. Actually, he was following the basketball scores scrolling along the bottom of the televised game on the screen. With the sound muted, Brianne had forgotten the set was on.

"Holly seems to be in a good space, don't you think?"

Gavin watched the replay of a jump shot hitting its target. "Yeah."

Brianne peeked around the corner of the bathroom to face him. "What was my question?"

He returned her gaze. "Something about Holly. She's a great kid." Most thoughts of his daughter brought a smile to his face. From the moment Holly first peeked at her excited new father, the two had enjoyed a special bond. Gavin insisted that her middle name be Brianne. Although Holly had his coloring, she had turned out to be so like his beautiful bride.

"Did you think Ty was unusually quiet tonight?" She brushed her strawberry curls circling her shoulders.

Gavin glanced at the screen, then back to his wife. "No more than usual, I suppose. Why are you asking?"

"He didn't have much to eat for dinner. Wonder if he's coming down with something?"

"Why don't you go take his temperature?" Gavin teased. "I'm sure a seventeen-year-old male would appreciate that attention from his mom."

"Oh, cut it out!" she teased back. "I know I worry about him too much. I just wish I could get through that dark cloud that seems to surround him."

"I know. So do I." Gavin motioned for Brianne to come sit on his side of the bed. She leaned toward him and planted a kiss on his forehead.

"A little lower," he suggested.

Brianne pulled back, laughing at her handsome husband. "That's gotten me in a lot of trouble through the years." She coughed, then stopped. "I think I'll go check on Ty. Maybe he really isn't feeling well."

"You're the one who isn't feeling well." Gavin watched as she left the room. The sound of coughing continued down the hall. He turned his attention back to the television.

Soon Brianne returned. "He's not there."

"Huh?" Gavin tried to gather his thoughts. "Maybe he went for a run. He does that a lot. You do know he's on the track team?"

"Very funny." Brianne walked to her side of the bed. "You're probably right." Carefully, she removed the prosthesis from her left stump and eased into bed.

"You're a remarkable woman." Gavin flicked off the remote and snuggled closer to her. He knew Brianne's genuine concern for her son was only part of her elevated anxiety level. In a couple of weeks, she would have a blood test and scans for any signs of cancer. He wanted to comfort her, but his pragmatic nature made him wonder why she always got into such a stew about her annual checkup.

She'd been a small child when her first cancerous tumor was removed. Her illness had brought her then recently divorced parents back together. Layton and Amy Brooks often shared how God had used Brianne's surgery to heal their marriage. However, after several years of remission, her cancer returned. Amputation of her left leg below the knee had given her back her life. She called her prosthesis a "trophy of grace." Instead of focusing on her loss, Brianne had counted every day of her life as gift.

She let out an uncharacteristic sigh. "I've got a bad feeling about this checkup, honey." Gavin pulled her even closer. "I take care of myself. I eat right, exercise, meditate, and get my rest. I follow doctor's orders, but I just can't shake my cough."

"Then let's do what we always do." They held hands as he led her in prayer, praising God for His tender care in the past and assurance of His love in the present—no matter the future.

Holly lowered her phone She wasn't tired, but she couldn't think of anything to do. She'd checked her social media sites throughout the evening. She'd talked to her on again/off again boyfriend in DC, but the call had upset her. She decided to share her feelings with Hannah Harper, her best friend from high school.

Because their first and last names began with the letter H, the two were known as "the 4H-ers." Although 4-H was actually an afterschool club, the tag stuck. In their circle of friends, the nickname was easier than trying to keep the friends' names straight—unless, of course, they purposefully mixed and matched them.

Mistaking the two for real would have been hard to do. Hannah was tall and slim with brown hair and hazel eyes. Far more studious than Holly, she was a quiet, reflective type who only occasionally added her words of wisdom to their group of friends. Holly loved her calming presence. Hannah could tease her impetuous friend into rethinking rash decisions.

The Harper family attended the same church, so the girls practically saw each other at least six days out of seven. Hannah had an older brother in the military and a younger one at home. After graduation, she had chosen to stay in Nashville and attend Peabody College of Vanderbilt University and major in secondary education.

Holly pressed the favorites button on her cell. When Hannah answered, Holly began, "Blake called—again."

"And hello to you, too," Hannah countered.

Ignoring the slight, Holly resumed. "His parents can't afford to fly him all the way to Los Angeles for Christmas. He's sitting alone in his apartment sulking and calling me every five minutes."

"I'm thinking that's a slight exaggeration. You do know how to let a call go to voicemail, right?"

"Oh, really? Who knew?"

"He's got a lot going for him."

"You know Dad doesn't like me dating a senior—even if he is an intern in Uncle Parker's DC office."

"Hmm … let me think." Holly could picture Hannah putting a finger to her cheek. "Blake Chandler. Sandy hair and green eyes. Muscular beach boy physique. Political science major. Hopes to get into an Ivy League law school next year. What's not to like?" She let the question hang. "What does your mom think?"

"She says I have a good head on my shoulders. She told my dad, 'Blake's the one you need to pray for. The way he's taken with Holly reminds me of someone I knew long ago.' Then I piped up, 'And how did that work out for you, Dad?'"

Hannah laughed. "So be sweet to Blake. You know Santa's keeping a list of who's naughty and nice."

"I can see you're no help," Holly concluded. "I'll see you at church tomorrow." The friends reviewed plans for Holly's birthday lunch on Christmas Eve and said goodnight.

Holly yawned and stretched. She looked at her stack of thank-you notes. Her mom always insisted she send handwritten notes before she used any of her birthday haul, including new clothes. Since Holly already knew who would give her presents, why not have the envelopes addressed?

Maybe a late-night run would revive her motivation. She ambled to the hallway. The light in her parent's bedroom was off, but Ty's burned brightly. She rapped softly on the door. When no one answered, she tried again. Slowly, she opened it, only to find the cluttered space empty.

Bet he's already out running, she thought. Probably the trail through the woods. Quickly, she returned to her room, donned her running shoes and a jacket, grabbed her phone and keys, and headed out the back door.

She'd never have ventured out this late at night in her DC neighborhood. But this was a gated community with a walking trail that maneuvered through the woods and across little rivulets of the Harpeth River behind the houses. Holly knew the path well.

As she rounded a turn, she saw a dim figure on a park bench some fifty yards ahead. Instinctively, she stopped, not sure who it might be and aware of her dark surroundings. Just as quickly, another figure approached the bench from the opposite direction. After a brief conversation, the two exchanged something. The second person headed back the way he had come. The person who had been sitting on the bench ran toward her. Holly ducked behind a tree.

When he passed her, Holly sucked in her breath. "Ty," she called. "Ty, wait for me."

Instead, the figure picked up speed. Determined to catch him, Holly sprang onto a footpath that cut the distance between them. "Ty, it's me, Holly," she panted.

Slowing down to a jog, Ty let her catch up to him. "What are you doing out here this late?" he grumbled.

"I could ask you the same question. Who were you meeting?"

"None of your business."

"Why so secretive? What's going on?"

Ty stopped and put his hands on his knees. His breathing slowed. "Why do you have to know everything?" he snapped. "I'm not your *little* brother anymore."

Holly tried to lighten the moment. She batted her eyelashes. "But I love you just as much."

Ty straightened himself. "Well … if you must know, he's a friend. You don't know him. We were … exchanging Christmas presents. He works late at a coffee shop, and we couldn't find any other time to meet."

Holly surveyed his slender frame. "So, where'd you put your present?"

"Knock it off, Holly. He gave me a gift card to buy a new video game. He didn't know what I liked." With that, Ty took off running at a speed Holly simply couldn't match.

By the time she reached the house, Ty's light was off. His ceiling fan purred through the closed door.

Strange. Very strange. Holly undressed and climbed into the shower, hoping the warm splashing water would wash away her concern. What she needed right now was the presence of the *Living Water*. Holly prayed for Ty and his friend. At least she hoped he was a friend.

3

The following two days brought intrigue and comfort for Brianne. Intrigue because she'd noted that Holly and Ty were mostly avoiding each other. Comfort because she had discovered her son's whereabouts on the night he'd not been in his room. Not overtly, of course. She knew better than to be a prying mother. But the subject came up when she saw a pile of smelly clothes and running shoes covered in muddy grass heaped on the floor at the end of his bed.

His explanation seemed plausible enough. In fact, she was relieved to know he had a friend—a friend close enough to exchange Christmas gifts with. When she'd mentioned it to Holly, her daughter shrugged, "I know," and left the kitchen with a handful of vegetable munchies. *Must not be a big deal,* Brianne surmised. But Holly's offhand remark seemed strange for a young woman known for over talking most any subject.

In fact, she'd been strangely preoccupied while the threesome had festooned the Christmas tree in the family room with mementoes dating back to each child's birth. Ty had come across the family Christmas album in the stack of boxes. Brianne always filled in the year's photos after the fact. Ty laughed at his pictures from the previous year, now that he'd grown several inches.

"Holly, thank goodness you cut your long hair for college. You looked like a twelve-year-old kid." Ty enjoyed the dig a little too much.

Always conscious of her size—or lack thereof—Holly snatched the book away. She flipped back toward the beginning of the book. "Let's find the photo of you playing with your rubber ducky in the bathtub." Ty turned a shade of crimson.

Their mother intervened and took the album away. "In a few days, I'll have new pictures of my two almost grown-up *children*." Her emphasis on the last word made the point. Whatever the cause of their spat, her children usually worked out their issues between them. After all, it was Christmas Eve, as well as Holly's big day. No time for squabbles.

After the kids had gone their separate ways, she put the finishing touches on the Christmas tree, adding mysterious packages beneath. She grinned at the clever system she'd invented when the children were small. She had discovered that little fingers were less likely to tamper with packages without names on them. All the packages were color-coded but the colors differed year by year. Only she possessed the code. The childhood tradition had become a family favorite.

Holly's birthday party later in the day would be a family affair. Holly knew Nana Amy and Grandpa Layton Brooks were coming, but Brianne hadn't breathed a word about the surprise guests. She grinned at the prospect of her daughter's reaction when the unexpected company appeared at the door.

Too bad her dad's brother Kyle wouldn't make it this year. He was unable to catch a flight out of Myanmar. And too bad Brianne had no siblings. But Parker and his wife Kathy were coming late in the afternoon. Kathy would help her put dinner on the table and then afterwards serve her sumptuous apple pie for anyone who had room to eat a piece. They'd miss Kathy's three children, now grown and scattered across the country. It seemed impossible that when Parker had married the widow, her kids had served as junior groomsman, flower girl, and ring bearer.

Brianne sat back on her knees. Gavin's family was accounted for. His father, Hollister Hamilton, had died ten years ago. And of course, Olivia and Alexis were in Italy. Not that they would have attended an informal family get-together. Olivia and Hollister had reared their sons and daughter in a house devoid of emotional connection. Alexis was just as aloof as her mother.

For twenty-plus years Brianne had prayed for this family. She knew the only lasting change would come from their embracing the gift of salvation, offered through Jesus' death on the cross. Sadly, Hollister had died without professing faith in Christ. She shuddered at the thought.

Meanwhile, she had a turkey to baste and just enough time for a soaking bath before the guests arrived. And two children who seemed strangely uncomfortable in each other's presence.

Holly sat curled with her phone on the papasan chair she'd had in her bedroom since childhood. She'd thanked Blake for his birthday wishes and clicked off the call. The guy was simply lonely. *Not my problem*, she decided, then felt badly that she hadn't sympathized with him more.

At her lunch date with Hannah, the subject came up. "You can't just break up with him," Hannah observed. "It's Christmas! Besides, you're a volunteer at your uncle's DC office. It'll be awkward seeing him there."

"And that's another problem," Holly countered. "Everyone thinks I'll just stay in Washington after graduation and work in 'the family business'—as everyone calls The Sloan Foundation."

"Well, won't you? Your mom's worked for it all your life, and your dad's the foundation's attorney."

"I'm holding out. I've got to see what else is out there," she said convincingly.

"Well, you've got three-and-a-half years at least to make a decision." Hannah picked up her fork and dived into her chicken salad. "So, what else is going on?"

Holly was off and running, describing her recent late-night encounter with Ty. "Why doesn't Ty's story add up? If the guy he met was a friend, why didn't they sit on the bench and talk? Why didn't he bring a gift? Who was he, anyway? And why did he come through the woods instead of the gate to our community? Any friend of Ty's would be welcomed at our home, day or night."

"That's a lot to absorb," Hannah admitted. "But you'll work it out. I have every faith in your solving this case!"

Holly wondered. Her natural curiosity had gotten her into many scrapes through the years. Like the time she fell down a laundry chute. Who knew where that door went?

But this incident was more than idle curiosity, more than a mystery she needed to solve. She had a feeling … women's intuition … or maybe the Spirit's leading?

Either way, she couldn't seem to let it go.

The Christmas Eve festivities were in full swing. Holly sat on the living room floor entertaining the guys with stories from the nation's capital. Parker and Ty occupied the couch while Gavin claimed the armchair nearest the front door. Brianne and Kathy had just come in from the kitchen when the doorbell rang. Brianne hurried to the door.

"Hello, Kitten," said her dad, calling his only child by the pet name she had acquired as a toddler. She kissed his cheek as she collected two dishes of food from her mother's overloaded arms.

"Hi, honey. Thanks." Nana began removing her scarf and jacket. "I'm starved. I hope you have something to eat!"

Holly spoke up from her seated position. "Nana, didn't we tell you we're fasting?" She winked in her grandparents' direction. "And Grandpa, what about those ten pounds you're always threatening to lose?"

"Not on your birthday," he grinned as he leaned to plant a kiss on Holly's forehead.

Kathy squeezed in between Parker and Ty on the couch while Nana and Grandpa Brooks took the loveseat. Brianne placed her mom's dishes on the dining room table. When the doorbell rang again, Gavin headed to the front door. "Holly," he shouted, "it's for you." He reclaimed his seat on the armchair.

"Oh, cool, another FedEx delivery." Holly sprang up and ran to the door. Ear-piercing screams followed.

Holly's screams continued unabated. Since the other guests knew the surprise, they reacted to the drama with smiles and nudges. Nana was the first to reach Holly.

"Why, if it isn't my mom and dad. What a pleasant surprise!" She grinned at the elderly couple outside the door. Her parents, Meme Jan and Papa Phil Dyer, stood enveloped by Holly's arms and unable to move.

When Nana finally extricated the Dyers from Holly's arms, she led them into the living room, where they received loving embraces from the rest of the family. Ty removed their coats, while Nana ushered her parents to the couch. Parker and Kathy pulled in chairs from the dining room while Ty took the armchair opposite his father.

"This is the best present ever," Holly sighed. She sat cross-legged on the rug between her great-grandparents, holding tightly to their hands. "Why didn't someone tell me you were coming?"

"Darling, at our age we don't make long-range plans," Meme Jan laughed. "When your mom sent us the plane tickets, all we promised was, 'we'll try.'"

"So how is sunny Florida?" Gavin asked.

"About eighty degrees," Papa laughed. "We keep busy. We still work with the Latinos in our church."

Meme chimed in, "Mostly, we serve as prayer warriors now. Is there anything greater than seeing God at work in the lives of those on your daily prayer list?" Heads nodded.

With dinner on the table, the group moved to the dining room. After dinner—and at least an hour of Holly's exuberance over each card and birthday present—they gathered around the Christmas tree in the family room. Long ago Holly had learned to share her birthday with Ty, who always got to open one present under the tree—that is, a color-coded present his mother would hand-pick from the pile.

Tonight, Brianne fairly gleamed as she handed a thin package to her son. Unlike his sister, Ty discarded the paper quickly and held up a book. Quizzically, he read aloud the title and author: *Set Free to Serve* by Parker Sloan Hamilton.

Everyone's attention turned to Parker, who looked like the cat who swallowed the canary. "It's not even in bookstores yet," he explained. "Just got a shipment from the publisher days ago. Hot off the press, Ty. You're my first reader."

Ty leaned over and gave his uncle a knuckle tap. "Th-thanks. I'm sure it's a great book."

The book quickly made its way around the circle of admirers. Parker explained that it contained testimonies from many of the men who had come through The Sloan Foundation's rehabilitation program—including his own story.

"Why didn't I get one?" Holly grumbled.

"You're forgetting about tomorrow," Parker grinned. "Another day, another round of gifts … Ty gets a head start because he's my favorite nephew."

"I'm your only nephew," Ty reminded.

"Well, that, too." Parker autographed the book and handed it to its new owner. Ty held it uncomfortably, as though it might contain explosives. A flicker of concern crossed Holly's face as she noted her brother's puzzling reaction to his uncle's book.

Meme glanced from Ty to Holly and back again.

The family shared a closing prayer, and the guests made their way to the door with coats in hand. Meme Dyer placed her arm around Holly's waist. "Something's troubling you," she whispered. "Whatever it is, God's up to something!"

Holly kissed her cheek. Meme could always read her moods. And she was always sure God was at work in every situation. Because, of course, He always is.

꙳

Ty shut down his iPhone and stared out the window. A full moon cast shadows on the trees behind the house. He had at least a half hour before … well, before he needed to change into his running shorts and shoes.

His glance fell on Uncle Parker's book where he had tossed it when he came back to his room after the Christmas Eve party. *Set Free to Serve. Weird title,* he thought. *What do freedom and service have to do with each other?*

Ty knew all about Parker's crime, his time in prison, and what had led him to open the first Sloan House years before Ty was born. Through a series of events in Parker's life, including his grandmother Sloan's surprising bequeath of her estate to him, he had opened a halfway house in east Nashville, just minutes from the downtown hangouts Ty's father Gavin had often visited.

From the time he was old enough to be taken out in public, Ty had listened to Parker's passionate speeches at fundraisers while his mom manned the registration table. He fingered the book. *What's the big deal, anyway?* he wondered. Parker hadn't been gang raped or knifed or kept in solitary confinement. He'd been released after his first parole hearing and had traveled the straight and narrow ever since.

What had been so bad about being the son of a wealthy family in exclusive Belle Meade, getting a medical degree from Vanderbilt, and inheriting his grandmother Sloan's estate? Somehow, Ty couldn't feel a lump in his throat when he thought about Parker's fall from riches to rags to riches again. Yet, Parker made his living by telling his "from prison to rehabilitation" story and getting others to buy into it—literally.

Sure, his uncle was a nice guy who meant well. But he was always full of these "testimonies," as he called the sad tales of the men in the various Sloan Houses across the nation. Ty wished Parker would get a life, or at least, leave others to live the one they had. If he heard another story about a cocaine overdose, he knew he'd puke.

Still, his eyes never left the book's cover. Slowly, he opened it, passed the title page, and stared at the dedication.

To my nephew Tyler
Who's never known the scourge of drugs or alcohol.
May it ever be so.

Ty caught his breath. How dare Parker use his name without his permission? He felt violated, as though the whole world would be watching his every move from now on. As if his staying away from substance abuse were the end all and be all of life.

Quickly, he changed into his running clothes. He left the house and jogged the trail toward the woods.

Across the hall Holly heard her brother's door close. *Ty's going for a run,* she assumed, but her heart skipped a beat. Should she follow him? Or, more accurately, should she follow him again?

Sunday night Holly had followed him. She had stealthily jogged at a slower pace behind him. To her relief, Ty had run the trail and come straight home. Her imagination was probably running wild. Maybe she was way too curious. Like the time she'd trailed her dad to the place he'd parked her high school graduation gift—her first new car.

Her dad knew she was right behind him. That was the joke: to get her to follow him in her older model Ford to where he'd parked her sports car on the vacant high school parking lot. Holly knew she'd been *had* when her mom and brother jumped from the backseat yelling, "Surprise."

No, Holly needed to chill. Her brother was OK. She was acting like a little mother hen. Besides, she was tired from the birthday party, especially the surprise of her great-grandparents' visit. Meme Dyer had picked up on the fact that something was worrying her. Sometimes Meme seemed connected to some otherworldly place in which she could read minds and hearts. Even on the telephone. Holly often teased her that she should have gone into fortunetelling.

Maybe she was just reacting to Nana's stories about Meme Dyer's spiritual insights. Ever since Meme and Papa had become Christians as adults, they had resembled the biblical couple Aquila and Priscilla, using their talents to minister to others. Back when Nana and Papa divorced, the Dyers were serving as volunteer missionaries to Ecuador.

Holly remembered they had come home just in time to witness their daughter Amy's transformation as a new Christian. Despite her divorce and her daughter Brianne's cancer surgery, Nana trusted God with her future. In that crisis experience Meme had first uttered the phrase now etched in the family's memory bank: "God's up to something."

Sure enough, He was. God worked a miracle of reconciliation between her grandparents, Layton and Amy Brooks, and—for several years—her mom's cancer remission. Later, while still a youngster, her mom lost part of her left leg to cancer. Meme was the first in the family to see the artificial limb as a trophy of grace.

That's how Holly's mom had come to terms with her loss. Every inquiry or look of curiosity from a new friend gave her an opportunity to witness to God's grace: His grace in salvation, in restoring her family and her life, and in using her as a testimony to others. Her mom's faith had definitely rubbed off on Holly.

At her birthday party, Meme had whispered to her, "God's up to something." If only Holly knew *what*.

Christmas morning arrived at last. After the family exchanged personal gifts, Gavin, Brianne, and Holly left for Parker and Kathy's home in East Nashville. Ty waited a few minutes and drove himself over. At these family gatherings a kid with his own car would be expected to come and go as he pleased.

Not that these events were boring, Ty admitted to himself as he drove. After the lunchtime feast, all the guys would play touch football while Papa Phil coached from the sidelines. After a light dinner, each would open one gift and then draw a name for the next year's celebration. Most were gag gifts, with an occasional sentimental ornament or "blast from the past."

Then they took turns reading the Christmas story and leading the prayer. The adults would chat and play cards and table games until bedtime. That would be his signal to leave. Unlike Holly, who liked the grown-up attention, he wasn't in to the totally outdated games of his grandparents' and great-grandparents' generations.

No, the day wouldn't be a mystery. But Ty liked the predictability. It made him feel safe.

He parked along the curb in front of the rambling brick house, built in the early 1900's when East Nashville served as the city's hub. Kathy had completely remodeled the charming Victorian and surrounded the front entrance with a curved landscaped driveway.

Before he could ring the bell, Holly opened the expansive oak door. Ty fumed, clearly irritated. "What are you, clairvoyant?"

"Hello sir, table for how many?" Holly pretended to hold pencil and paper, as though she were the hostess at a posh restaurant.

Ty brushed past her and into the massive foyer. The family was gathered in the family room to his left. The lively conversation seemed to be centered on Parker's book—a subject Ty didn't care to discuss. He was still smarting from the dedication page. Before he could plan his escape up the staircase to the game room at the top of the stairs, he heard Nana call his name.

Reluctantly, Ty joined the group, pulled to the couch between Nana and Grandpa. Nana grabbed his hand. "Did you see the dedication page, Tyler?"

"Yeah, I saw it." Ty looked down at the Oriental rug at his feet.

"Wasn't that sweet? I've never had a book written to *me*." Nana cocked her head and winked at Parker.

Ty was uncomfortable being the center of attention. Noting his discomfort, his mom diverted the conversation. "Parker, why don't you read the part about your brother, my loving husband?"

"No, no, please," groaned Gavin. "Not before lunch."

Just then Kathy rang the dinner bell—literally—the one hanging over the kitchen island. Everyone lined up for the buffet meal. Ty straggled to the back of the line, which, it turned out, Parker had reserved for himself as the host.

Ty knew he should say something to Parker about the book—at least about the dedication—but the words stuck in his throat. Finally, he muttered, "Nice cover, Uncle Parker."

"Glad you like it." Parker laid a familiar hand on his shoulder. "One of the guys at The Sloan House drew the initial concept. Of course, your mom had the final say."

Standing in front of Ty, Grandpa overheard the remark and added, "I've always teased my Kitten about her take charge ways."

"Where'd she inherit that from?" Parker teased.

Just then, Kathy called him to retrieve a heavy pan from the oven. Ty breathed a sigh of relief.

It wasn't that he didn't like his uncle. Everybody liked Parker. He had a heart of gold, always helping someone, bringing hope to discouraged family members of druggies. The recidivism rate for The Sloan House was far below average.

His discomfort was more about their differences. Parker was outgoing and goal-oriented. Ty was painfully shy and unsure of his place in the world. Standing inches taller than Ty, Parker was an imposing figure who kept in shape and seemed relentlessly in pursuit of a godly life.

Who could live up to that? he wondered. Parker was the family star, the leader, the one with the story to tell and the life to be emulated. All of which made Ty feel inferior and unremarkable.

He reached the buffet just as Holly returned for a hot roll. She raised her eyebrows. "Already back for seconds?" If looks could kill, his sister would be a dead woman.

6

Before Ty left Parker's house Christmas evening, Kathy's kids had arranged to be on Zoom. He'd had a chance to talk to his cousins. He missed the Collins' kids, especially Matt, who was closest to Ty's age.

Kathy's children had always been a part of Ty's life. Christmas just felt different without David, Gina, and Matt. Although as children they'd lived across town and gone to different schools, Matt was the older brother Ty had never had. Ty had grown up seeing them at least weekly at church.

It was the same church where Layton Brooks had grown up, taken Amy as a young bride, and reared their daughter Brianne. Uncle Parker had joined after he became the director at a medical center in Nashville. Later, a layman in the church, Layton Brooks, became his mentor.

Then when Ty's father became a Christian, Gavin began attending as well. Ty could repeat by heart his father's story about "that Brooks girl dragging me to church kicking and screaming." But he, too, had raised his children in the same church. Holly and Ty had each been infants in the church nursery.

The family's longtime pastor, Frank Norwell, had retired several years ago and now resided in assisted living. His presence during all their family's major events had left a deep impression on Ty. Often, he'd thought about talking to Pastor Frank, just as his father, uncle, and grandfather had done when life loomed larger than their faith.

But it wasn't possible. Not when the whole church thought his family was picture-perfect, when his older sister had been the standout star of the church's youth group. When she left for college, he thought he'd find his place in the group—his identity.

Instead, he realized that Holly had been his support system, his protector and defender, the one who insisted Ty be invited to everything the group planned. He still didn't know how to find his own way in social situations. He knew he needed to stand on his own two feet—if only he could find them.

Ty's car moved slowly through the downtown Christmas Day traffic. Watching the crowds move from restaurants and bars to music venues on the festive streets, he felt even lonelier. Where was he going? It had seemed important to leave Parker's house early, as though he had somewhere to go, something to do, someone to meet. Leaving would make him seem normal—a teenager bored with adults and out to have a good time with friends.

In fact, he had no plans for the evening. Driving aimlessly seemed pointless. With the touch of a button, he connected with Guillermo Sanchez. "Hey, William?" he asked.

"Guillermo, to you, gringo. ¿Señor, como usted esta?"

"Bien. What are you up to?"

"¿Eres de verdad, hombre?"

Ty could hear commotion in the background. His friend explained, "It's Christmas. All my relatives are here."

"Where's 'here'? he asked.

¿Aqui? We had to rent Music City Center to get them all in."

Ty chuckled. Guillermo often joked about his large extended family. "OK, I get it," he said. "You're busy. I'll let you get back to the fiesta."

"If you want to come over, I'm sure we can find a half-eaten tamale."

"No, I'll catch you later. Merry Christmas."

"Feliz Navidad."

The line went dead. Ty directed the car toward home. He should have known Guillermo would be surrounded by relatives. He was that kind of guy. The two had met in his sophomore math class. Guillermo was struggling with algebra equations, and Ty was having trouble in Spanish. A perfect match. Since then, they'd hung together at lunch and occasionally caught a movie or a ballgame.

Now Ty could hold his own in Spanish. He'd not done much with his new language skills, but he enjoyed the mental gymnastics of keeping up a bilingual conversation—a knack that came easy for Guillermo. In fact, his friend rarely completed a sentence without using both languages.

He turned into his driveway and, gloating that Holly's car was still in DC, pulled into the third spot of the three-car garage. He headed for the kitchen door and another night of —what? Once in his room, he threw his keys on the nightstand and sprawled across his bed.

Ty heard Holly and his parents return home around 10:30 p.m. Quickly, he picked up his iPhone and began checking YouTube for new postings. He needed to at least appear to be doing something. Soon Holly knocked on his door.

"Come in ... but don't step on anything."

"Then I can't come in!" Holly quipped. She sidestepped a pile of clothes, talking as she entered. "The 'old folks' couldn't take it anymore. I won practically every game we played."

"Wow! Too bad I missed it," he groaned. "Maybe someone posted it on Instagram."

"Cute. Real cute. You would've had a great time, Ty. Papa told a bunch of funny stories about their years in Ecuador. Of course, Meme had to correct him on most of them ..."

Ty's cell beeped, interrupting Holly mid-sentence. He hadn't expected a text at this hour on December 25th. Ty glanced at the phone.

"Hey, what's up?" Holly plopped down on his bed.

As he pushed the off button, Ty glared at his sister. "None of your business. And even if it were, I wouldn't tell you."

Holly opened her mouth—but no words came out. She pulled her knees to her chest.

"Sorry. I didn't mean it that way." Ty felt trapped. "I just don't like how you think you should know everything I do."

Holly gave him a penetrating gaze. She slowly stood and marched across the hall to her room. Ty felt worse than ever. He kicked at the pile of clothes on the floor and uttered a few whispered self-recriminating words as he shut his door.

Ty sat quietly on the bench, listening for footsteps on the gravel path. When a lone figure emerged from the shadowy trail, he moved to make a place for the visitor to sit.

A few minutes later, Ty rose from the bench and jogged toward home while the other person walked quickly in the opposite direction.

Once home, lying on his bed fully clothed, he waited for his heartbeat to settle to a normal rhythm. He had to plan his next move.

Holly heard her brother come in. With great forethought, she had moved a kitchen chair just the slightest bit so he'd bump into it on his way from the back door through the kitchen into the hallway. That way she'd be sure to hear him bump the chair on the tile floor.

At least he's alive and walking, she thought. Seconds went by. She glanced at her phone screen. Seven minutes until midnight. Nothing too mysterious happened before midnight—at least in movies. Ty hadn't been gone long enough to get in any serious trouble.

Why am I so worried about him, she wondered. *Maybe I should get up and look for the trail of blood on the kitchen floor.* She chided herself for being so melodramatic. Simple curiosity, that's all it was. She pulled the covers around her shoulders. Sleep would come, but not before she thanked her heavenly Father for her brother's safe return.

7

Brianne snuggled into her favorite spot on the window seat in her bedroom. The warm throw around her feet and a cup of steaming coffee took the chill off the room. Gavin had just left for a breakfast meeting with a young father he was mentoring. Ty wouldn't be up for another hour or so. Holly? Heaven only knew when she'd wake up.

The Christmas festivities had been fun, but she was ready for a break. Yesterday Holly and Ty had helped her take down the decorations displayed throughout the house. They always left the family room, with its beautiful tree and mementoes scattered across the branches, until after the New Year. Every year she seemed to collect additional holiday knickknacks, so she'd been glad for their help. Now the house resembled the comfortable place she'd designed piece by piece with her mother's eye for style and function.

Brianne loved having Holly home and secretly hoped none of the part-time jobs she'd applied for would open. After all, she only had a little over three weeks left before the next school term—hardly enough time to earn any serious cash. Besides, it would cost a business too much to do the paperwork to hire her. Still, neither parent had tried to talk Holly out of the job search. Holly was on a quest, and her stubborn persistence wouldn't be denied.

Although Brianne knew her hours at The Sloan Foundation had been cut, she didn't stop the work flow simply because Parker could no longer afford her full salary. The effort to keep the foundation running smoothly required unpaid time in her home office. However, she really didn't mind because the work of the foundation was part of her DNA. She couldn't sacrifice the futures of hundreds of recovering addicts by working less—any more than Parker could.

Surely, Holly's stellar instincts must have picked up something odd. Didn't she realize Christmas wasn't as elaborate this year? Soon Holly would want to make plans for their annual shopping bonanza—normally a days-long affair. Even in the best of times, the Hamilton women shopped the after Christmas sales. Holly's sleuthing would uncover hidden gems under the piles of sale items, and she'd proudly announce the savings to her budget-conscious father.

Brianne sipped her coffee and picked up the Bible lying beside her. She read several familiar psalms of comfort, assuring her of her Father's faithfulness. Then she turned to Romans 8 to saturate her mind in God's promise to never leave her side. In fact, nothing could separate her from Him—not even her annual pilgrimage to the doctor's office later in the day.

She knew she'd been coughing a lot recently. To her family she passed it off as simply the result of winter weather and all the respiratory ailments that went with it. She sensed Gavin wanted to believe her story and would gladly shy away from the subject. Still, the worry wouldn't go away. He was meeting her at 2 p.m. at Dr. Ted Poole's office in the midtown medical center.

Dr. Poole had been the family's internist for as long as she could remember. Parker had gone to medical school with him. Later—after Parker's release from supervised parole—Ted had helped him get his medical license restored and offered him the position of medical director at a nonprofit clinic near downtown Nashville. After three years there, Parker had opened The Sloan House and set up the foundation he now ran.

All of which was made possible by his inheritance from Gram Sloan, Olivia Hamilton's mother—which came as a total surprise. Parker's father, Hollister Hamilton, a prominent Nashville lawyer, had fought Parker's efforts to claim the money since Gram had made it clear in her will that Parker would have to demonstrate that he had been rehabilitated. Since she didn't live to see that happen, Parker's fitness had to be determined by a court.

The fact that Hollister lost the lawsuit had only hardened his heart against his son. Olivia, of course, had kept her crystalline poise through the whole ordeal, refusing to let the controversy interfere with her social and charitable endeavors. Only Parker seemed to suffer from the rebuff.

Although Brianne hadn't known Parker or Gavin at the time of the trial, she certainly knew its impact on her family. Her father-in-law had died without the Lord from a sudden heart attack when Holly was nine and Ty almost eight. She was glad her children were too young to clearly remember him. *Let the dead bury the dead.*

Brianne dropped to her knees and prayed for each family member by name and for peace for herself—peace that would certainly have to pass her present understanding.

Holly buckled her seat belt. Spending the afternoon with Nana Amy and Meme Jan had been a wonderful idea. The visit would help take her mind off her mom's appointment with Dr. Poole. Besides, she couldn't think of a place she'd rather be than Nana's house.

Holly could visualize every nook and cranny of the house where her mother had grown up. She knew every tree, bush, and flowerbed. She had romped through the grass with Harvey, now buried beneath the oak tree at the back of the lot. (Who knew codes didn't allow dogs to be buried on the premises? No one had the heart to dig up old Harvey.)

She parked at the curb and climbed the steps to the porch. Through the blinds of the picture window, she saw Meme Jan grinning from ear to ear. Nana opened the door.

"Hi, hon." She began gathering her purse and woolen wrap off the chair nearest the door. "As it turns out, I've got to run. There's an issue with the condo I've styled for tomorrow's open house. I'll be back in an hour or so. Meme promised to play nice!"

"Oh, I never said that," the older woman chuckled. "Holly and I are going to think up some major mischief while you're gone."

Nana smiled. "Holly doesn't need any help with mischief." She gave them both a quick peck on the cheek and shut the front door behind her.

Meme's eyes twinkled. "So, shall we shuffle furniture from room to room or trade out all the pictures on the walls?"

Holly giggled. "No, let's visit instead. Shall I put on a pot of tea?"

Instead of waiting for an answer, she headed for the kitchen. "Where are Grandpa and Papa?"

"At the YMCA. I think Phil is on his second lap in the pool about now. Layton's probably on his fourth or fifth."

When the teacups were filled, Holly and Meme assumed their places at the kitchen table. A comfortable silence ensued as they sipped the warm cranberry orange herbal mixture. Holly stared out the bay window at a mulberry bush shaking off the last of a wintry frost. "Meme, do you think Mom's going to be OK?"

When her great-grandmother didn't respond, Holly glanced in her direction, then down at her cup. "I know, Meme. 'Don't borrow trouble.' But I'm worried."

Finally, Meme spoke. "You want me to tell you not to worry?"

"Of course not." Holly paused. "I just want you to listen to me while I worry."

Meme sighed. "How many years has the Lord given your mom since that first diagnosis of cancer? I try to remember to thank Him every day for my only grandchild. And my two precious great-grandchildren," she added with a twinkle. "And I'll ask Him again, with the faith that moves mountains, to spare Brianne. But our days are numbered, sweet Holly, and I have to leave the answer in His hands."

Tears trickled down Holly's cheeks. "That's easy for you to say! She's not your mother. And you're not nineteen and scared to death." She brushed the tears away.

"No child, Brianne is not my mother, and I'm not nineteen." Meme leaned back in her chair. "You didn't know Myra Norwell," she began.

"I know of her," Holly sniffed. "Pastor Frank's wife. She died when my mom was a child. The church media center is named for her."

Meme continued as though her train of thought hadn't been interrupted. "Now, there was a woman of faith. She struggled with her cancer diagnosis. 'Why me?' she asked. And then she looked around at the other patients in the cancer treatment center and asked, 'Why not me?'

"Your Nana Amy and Myra were quite close, you know. How many times have I heard Amy quote Myra: 'Suffering is an equal opportunity employer. But it offers the privilege of fellowship with Christ's suffering and God's power made perfect in weakness.'"

Meme sat up straight. "You probably think I'm talking like an old woman who's eager to go be with Jesus." Her eyes settled on Holly. "But I'm telling you, God's up to something in this family, and He's always good. He doesn't know how to be any other way."

Gavin clicked off his cell phone and stood in the hallway outside an examining room. He'd had to take the call, but now he needed to get back to Brianne. Dr. Poole would return with some preliminary results any minute.

He was glad Brianne had been honest with the doctor about her cough. Inwardly, however, he kicked himself for previously having been so ready to accept her explanation. *Why do men in general, and me in particular, work so hard to avoid bad news? We're supposed to be men of courage. Right now, I feel like the jelly I put on my toast this morning.*

When he opened the door, he found Brianne leaning back against the papered exam table with her eyes tightly closed. She looked up at him just as a stray tear tricked down one cheek. Gavin moved toward her. She sat up and they embraced.

"I'm scared, honey."

"I know." He patted her back as he had once done for his children's skinned knees or bruised egos. Words seemed inadequate.

Still in that position, they heard Dr. Poole knock and quickly enter the room. He carried several X-rays and her chart. He took a position beside the small desk where he wrote his prescriptions. Then he positioned an X-ray on the wall hooks.

Pointing to the X-ray, he showed her a speck on her right lung. "We want to get this checked out. I'm sending you downstairs for an MRI. I'll have the results in the morning. Meanwhile, I'm referring you to a lung specialist in our clinic. My nurse will make you an appointment before you leave."

"So," Gavin inquired, "do you think this is serious?"

Dr. Poole looked at Brianne. "With your history, we have to take every precaution. We need to rule out cancer."

Before he left, Dr. Poole led them in prayer, asking for God's wisdom and His one-of-a-kind comfort as they awaited next steps.

Gavin settled Brianne in her favorite recliner in the family room. He picked up his cell phone to call Brianne's parents. She'd asked him to make the call, though it would break their hearts. She couldn't deal with their sorrow and her own. Trying to lighten the mood, she told him, "It's why I married a steely-eyed lawyer with a reputation for toughness."

"My façade is breaking apart," he confessed. "I feel like a bowl of gelatin." Nonetheless, he made the call. Fortunately, Layton answered. Having shared so much with his former mentor, Gavin talked, cried, and prayed his way through the conversation, leaving his father-in-law to break the news to his wife, Amy.

Moments after disconnecting, his cell rang. When the caller ID showed Parker's name, he clicked to answer.

"Hey, bro," Parker said. "Do you have a minute?"

"Yes, but …"

"Good. I just got off the phone with Alexis. Mother is on her way home from Italy."

"Huh. I thought she'd stay longer." Gavin stationed a throw pillow in the small of his wife's back and clicked the phone to speaker.

"Here's the deal." Parker was in his no-nonsense mode, speaking rapidly. "When she arrives, her driver will take her directly to Vanderbilt Hospital. She's checking in on the advice of her doctor here. They teleconferenced about her symptoms."

Gavin didn't say anything. With the afternoon's news about Brianne still weighing heavily, he couldn't quite compute the information.

Parker kept talking. "Mom's congestive heart failure seems to have worsened. Alexis thinks she'll be in the hospital several days. Her doctor wants to run some tests—maybe replace her pacemaker. Alexis wants us to check on her."

Gavin frowned. This must be serious. His mother normally didn't want visitors when she was not at her best. He couldn't imagine that she would have asked for her sons' attention. And his sister's request seemed out of character for both of the fiercely independent Hamilton women.

"The thing is," Parker continued, "I've got two back-to-back fundraisers in Detroit, and then we're opening The Sloan House in Omaha this weekend. Kathy's with me. We'll be on the road for the next five days."

"I'll look in on her," Gavin responded. He jotted down the information about her flight. "Parker … we got some troubling news about Brianne today."

Parker seemed to stop breathing. He and Brianne were closer than brother- and sister-in-law. They'd worked together for longer than Gavin had known his wife.

"She's got a spot on her right lung. Dr. Ted doesn't know what that means yet, but she's had an MRI, and he's sending her to a lung specialist. I don't mind telling you, we're worried."

After a long pause, Parker replied, "Bro, I'm truly sorry. I wish I could do something. To coin a phrase, when it rains, it pours, huh? Lousy timing. Maybe I should ask Alexis to come home."

Gavin thought about it. "That's probably a good idea, but for now I'm sure Holly and Amy and even Meme Jan can look in on Mother. Brianne and I will do what we can."

"I know." Parker sounded very tired.

"Just go make some money for the foundation," Gavin said. "That will do as much as anything to bolster Brianne's spirits. Keep us in your prayers, and we'll do likewise."

"Love you, man. Give my love to Brianne." With that, the brothers clicked off. Gavin turned to Brianne to hear her reaction.

The following day Grandmother Sloan arrived at Vanderbilt and settled into the suite she'd arranged there. Brianne felt someone should at least check on her, and Holly seemed the obvious choice. However, talking her daughter into the proposition proved to be tough.

"I don't want to go!" Holly crossed her arms. "I want to stay here with you." She leaned her elbows on the kitchen island.

"I know you do, but there's really nothing you can do for me right now, and I don't see the specialist for another week."

"I don't even really know Grandmother Hamilton," Holly retorted. "She's been like, like this 'touch me not' person all my life. What am I supposed to say? 'Well, Granny dear, you look lovely in your hospital gown.'"

"Holly, you're angry. I think we all are. And now you're supposed to show concern for someone who's made herself a stranger to you. It's unfortunate. I'm really sorry."

"But, why me?"

"Because Gavin is in court today. Because I have this cough, and I don't think I'd be welcomed in a hospital room. Because Ty's at track practice …"

"I get that." Holly reached for her coat. "I just needed a little temper tantrum."

Brianne laughed. "Come here, you big baby!" She hugged her daughter tightly. "You go make your grandmother's day a little brighter. We'll all be together this evening."

As Holly moved away, she looked back at her mom, wishing away the circumstances all of them faced. Once tightly buckled in her mom's car, Holly prayed, "Dear God, here I am thinking of myself when Grandmother doesn't even have You in her life. Give her time, Lord. Time to make her peace with You."

At the hospital Holly stood outside her grandmother's hospital room waiting on a nurse to finish checking her vitals. She thought about her first impressions of her stately grandmother, when, as an adventurous preschooler, she'd often received disapproving glances. Strangely, she could never remember being reprimanded by her. The expression on Olivia Hamilton's face served as more than an adequate deterrent for her childish antics.

She pictured her grandmother as a beautiful woman, coiffed and styled to perfection. Holly had wanted to please her more than anything—and to touch the jeweled necklaces and painted nails and run her chubby fingers over her smooth cheeks. But Olivia held everyone at bay, including her grandchildren. She remembered hearing Uncle Parker refer to her once as "chiseled marble."

Her grandmother had always been exceedingly polite and appropriately generous with cards and money—things that took the place of real relationship. Holly sighed, imagining the cool reception she'd get once she entered the room.

A nurse brushed past her on her way out of the room. Bracing herself, Holly stepped inside.

9

As the sound of Holly's footsteps echoed off the tile floor, Olivia turned her head slightly, then looked puzzled when she saw Holly.

"Hello, Grandmother." Holly stood awkwardly beside the bed.

"Hello, my dear. I wasn't expecting you."

"No … I—uh, Mom and Dad are tied up today, and Uncle Parker and Aunt Kathy are out of town. I came to ask if I could do … get you something …" Holly trailed off, uncomfortable with her explanation.

"Why, that's very kind of you dear. Come closer, would you?"

Holly shuffled a foot or so closer to the head of the bed. Her grandmother looked smaller than she remembered. Not the commanding figure who could silence her with a look. Instead, frail and vulnerable. Her silvery hair still fell in waves around her lovely face. Holly felt a childish urge to run her finger across her soft cheeks, much as she'd wanted to as a small child.

Holly tried to recall the last time she'd seen her. Had she come to her high school graduation tea? She tried to picture her in the buzz of her friends' chatter. Maybe she'd just dropped off a gift. Grandmother was speaking—

"You're quite beautiful—so grown up now."

Holly blushed. She'd not expected a compliment. This slightly warmer than anticipated reception left her more tongue-tied.

After a pause, the older woman spoke. "Did you, perhaps, drive yourself here?

"Yes, ma'am."

"I would like to ask a favor, if I may."

Holly nodded.

"Louisa and Clarissa weren't expecting my return from my trip quite yet. I'd given them two more weeks of vacation."

Holly had known her housekeeper and cook since birth. She nodded again.

"Since you're here, would you fetch a few things from my house for me?"

Holly brushed aside her mental picture of the foreboding mansion. "Why, of course."

"My driver took my luggage there. But I'd like to have some of my things. I really don't want to send him back for them. I don't like the idea of his going through my intimates. Perhaps I'm being foolish."

"Do—do you want me to go for them? Now?"

"Yes, dear. I'd like that very much." She retrieved her security code and house key from the purse Holly handed her. She made a list on the back of a hospital menu sheet with complete instructions as to where the items she wanted were located. Then she closed her eyes. "I'm quite tired from my trip. Jet lag, you know."

Holly couldn't remember when she had last been in the Belle Meade house. The brick structure was as imposing as ever, with its white columned porch and massive wooden door. She parked her car in the covered circular drive, unlocked the front door, and quickly entered the security code.

The polished hardwood staircase to the left led to the second floor. She climbed the stairs and passed what had been Gram Sloan's suite many years ago. Holly had no idea what the rooms were used for now. Olivia never entertained overnight guests. At least she'd never heard of any.

Holly looked over the banister to the foyer and into the immense drawing room beyond it. Turning her eyes back to the second floor, she walked past a hallway to her left that led to the rooms of each of the three Hamilton children. Although it was mid-morning, the hall was dark and musty-smelling. Holly shivered. She continued straight ahead and stopped at her grandmother's suite. Just beyond its door, a back staircase led to the downstairs.

Slowly, she opened the bedroom door, not quite sure what she would find. Holly tried to recall having been in there before, but no memories surfaced. Across the room, light blue tie-back curtains outlined the French doors that opened to a deck. The matching blue and tan colors in the bed furnishings and sitting area were obviously the work of an experienced interior decorator, but the room felt dated with its matching mahogany furniture. It lacked any personal touches. No family pictures. No books on the nightstand. Nothing that would indicate the personality of the woman who lived there.

She found her grandmother's travel suitcase in the middle of the massive walk-in closet where the driver had obviously placed it. Finding a smaller version stacked against an interior wall, she opened both pieces and began transferring items from the list. She worked quickly, uncomfortable invading Grandmother's private space. Then she entered the master bath and gathered a few things from counters and drawers. Once the list was completed, she paused in front of the king-sized bed, glanced around the room as though she might never see it again, and exited the second floor carrying the overnight case.

She set it by the front door. How long had it been since she was here? Possibly not since her grandfather had died. Maybe she had time to explore the rest of the house. She wandered into the foyer—immaculate, tasteful, but lifeless. To her left beneath the stairwell a door led to her grandfather's study. Filled with large mahogany furniture, a settee and high-backed chairs, the room was imposing but sterile. Across the foyer, the sprawling drawing room with its massive brick chimney and numerous sitting areas had seen its share of cocktail parties. Now it lay quiet, stilled by years of non-use.

A crooked grin crossed her face when she entered the dining room, the scene of so many of Parker's tales of woe. Grandfather Hollister had delighted in spending family meals cross-examining his older son, who rarely performed to his father's expectations. In the same room where Parker had endured so much misery, her father, Gavin, the younger brother, had been allowed to sing, play with his food, or concoct any tomfoolery that a spoiled brat could imagine. Holly smiled at her mental image of her father wildly swinging his feet under Grandmother's table.

Holly moved to the kitchen, where Clarissa ran a tight ship. The cabinets and countertops looked a bit dated now, but the room smelled of pleasant spices and a whiff of pine cleaner. She remembered many hours of Clarissa's chatter, as she would bake something special for Holly and Ty. Holly had made her very first cake in this room. At least she'd mixed the ingredients under Clarissa's watchful gaze while her parents and grandparents made small talk in the small parlor off the study.

Her eyes caught the rays of the late morning sun emanating from the pond in the immense backyard. She opened the French doors and wandered onto the stone patio where the Hamiltons had entertained governors, held wedding receptions, and hosted fundraisers for dozens of charities. Holly remembered Louisa's focused gaze as the two grandchildren played among the tables and chairs, chased butterflies, and captured unwitting frogs along the pond.

Charged with watching the children, Louisa kept them close to the house and always in view. Little did she know how terrified Holly and Ty would have been if they had played outside without her careful supervision. Now, from the vantage point of nineteen years, the yard seemed to have shrunk in size.

Having recalled the only good memories she could think of, she walked back into the house, locking the French doors behind her. At the entry she set the security code, picked up the overnight case, and cast a backward look at what had been a grand mansion in its day. She locked the massive door. Once in the car, she let out a long sigh and drove away.

Grandmother's pleasure at having "her things" surprised Holly. Did she, after all, have feelings? Did she attach meaning to the stuff of everyday existence? Was that cool, calculated exterior simply her way of playing the childhood game of keep away?

Mostly, Holly was taken aback at her grandmother's genuine look of gratitude. She wondered, *does anyone do her a favor without the exchange of money or another kind of gratuity?* She unpacked the case and put away its contents.

She left the hospital room without the usual sense of relief she'd often felt once out of her grandmother's presence. A flicker of compassion, even tenderness, flitted across her heart as she headed for the elevator. And a prayer. "God, once again, offer Grandmother Your peace, Your joy, Your assurance that she can spend her last days and all eternity with You."

10

Jan Dyer sat quietly in the hospital room, listening to Olivia's irregular breathing. She'd volunteered for this assignment, hoping to have an opportunity to visit with her granddaughter Brianne's mother-in-law, a woman older than her daughter Amy. The thought made her feel like an antique, having outlasted Claire Brooks and Gram Sloan—her contemporaries. For whatever reason in God's eternal plan, she was the one here, waiting on her part in the drama of Olivia Sloan Hamilton's life.

After a few minutes, a nurse came to check vitals, and Olivia awoke with a start. When the nurse left the room, Jan introduced herself. She'd only seen Olivia a few times—first, at Brianne's wedding, a second time at Hollister's funeral, when, coincidentally, he had died while the Dyers were visiting Nashville from their home in Florida. A third occasion occurred at a Christmas family gathering. Olivia's driver dropped her by Parker's home to deliver gift cards to her grandchildren and step-grandchildren—Kathy's three from her first marriage. Of course, she couldn't stay long—or so she said.

Olivia responded to Jan's introduction with well-bred but impersonal manners, thanking her for stopping by. Clearly ruffled by not looking her best, Olivia picked up her brush lying on the bedside tray and combed her silver hair. Jan was surprised by the woman's pale complexion and slender frame. Without the trappings of cosmetics, professionally styled hair, and a trendy wardrobe, Olivia was hardly the fashion showpiece of her previous encounters.

Immediately, Jan's heart went out to the frail woman. With Louisa and Clarissa out of town, she had no one to turn to except the family she had worked so hard to keep away. "Is there anything I can get you?" Jan asked kindly.

"Some water, please." After Jan poured it and handed her the plastic cup, Olivia asked, "And what brings you to Nashville?"

"The Christmas holidays. Phil and I were surprise guests at Holly's nineteenth birthday party."

Olivia furrowed her brow, trying to piece the words together. Having been in Italy, then suddenly forced back home with breathing problems, the days and times jumbled together in her mind. She nodded in Jan's direction as she sipped her drink. "I'm sure your family has been glad to see you. ...Weren't you overseas for a number of years? Somewhere in South America?"

"Yes, Phil and I were in beautiful Ecuador, working with a mission group sponsored by our church."

Olivia looked puzzled, as though the words had no meaning to her. But, resigned to Jan's presence, she set the paper cup back on the tray and lay back on her pillow. "Sounds interesting."

Jan breathed a quick prayer. She had hoped for an opportunity, and now God was giving her a chance to share His love. She quickly explained the nature of their work. Above all, she stressed their love for the native people.

"One characteristic of the Ecuadorians we noticed right away was their complacency with their life circumstances. Their religion compelled them to accept their lot in life as God's plan for them. They had no motivation to change or improve their situations or relationships."

Olivia lifted an eyebrow. Jan continued, "Our faith teaches us that God is always at work in our lives, seeking to bring us closer to Him. Getting to know God always involves change as we grow in likeness to His Son Jesus Christ. God even supplies the power for such change through the work of the Holy Spirit in our lives. Without the Spirit living inside of us, we'd be no more successful than the unsaved people of Ecuador."

Although Olivia had closed her eyes, her body movements indicated she wasn't asleep, so Jan plowed on. "Because God loves each of us so much, and because He knew none of us could be good enough to stand in His presence, He paid the price for our sins. He chose to sacrifice His only Son, Jesus, to bear the punishment we all deserve. All we have to do is ask His forgiveness and accept His Son's gift of eternal life."

Olivia nodded, but it was apparent she was drifting off to sleep. Jan lifted her eyes and praised her heavenly Father for the chance to plant seeds of faith. "God's up to something," she whispered, as she gathered her things and headed for the hallway.

Brianne's turn came the following day. A different cough suppressant made it possible for her to feel up to a trip to see her mother-in-law. No one had told Olivia about the spot on her lung, and she didn't want the news to burden a seriously ill family member.

Olivia was finishing lunch as she entered. Brianne spent the first few minutes helping her fill out her choices for dinner, clear away the tray, and brush her teeth. By now Olivia realized she had little independence and accepted the help of those who came to see her without much fuss.

Brianne asked about her visit to Alexis in Italy. Then, she kept the family news short and simple, aware that Olivia had little interest in details of their comings and goings. She did seem to perk up at the reminder of Parker's travels. An uncomfortable silence began to fill the space between them.

Finally, Olivia spoke up. "Your grandmother was here yesterday. I'm afraid I fell asleep on her."

Brianne assured her that Meme Jan understood completely. "I'll bet she was telling you about her work in Ecuador. She and Papa Phil are always eager to talk about their adventures overseas. You know, they went there to share Christ with the mountain people."

"I remember," Olivia murmured. "You know, our family used to attend church quite regularly when Alexis and Parker were young." Brianne remembered Parker's recollections of his mischievous actions during the pastor's homilies and Louisa's shoulder pinches that made church attendance a literal "pain in the neck."

She fell silent, during which Brianne prayed for God's guidance.

Finally, she spoke again. "Parker and Gavin changed a lot after they started attending your church. What was your pastor's name?"

"Frank Norwell. He's retired now."

"Yes, yes, that's it. I believe he had a tremendous influence on them. Your father, too."

"Yes, he mentored both of them."

"Thank him for that." Olivia sighed. "I'm glad their lives have worked out well." She nonchalantly asked, "And how is your health?"

Unprepared for that question, Brianne stammered until it became apparent that she was incapable of pulling off a falsehood. "Actually, I'll be seeing a lung specialist in a few days. I have a spot on my right lung."

"Oh, my," exclaimed Olivia. "Does this have anything to do with your previous bouts of cancer?"

"Possibly," Brianne conceded.

"And how do you feel about that?"

Again, Brianne was taken aback. Never had her mother-in-law sought to explore her feelings about anything. She remembered Meme's insistence that "God's up to something." She truthfully responded, "I'm nervous and a little depressed … but confident that if it's lung cancer, the disease is treatable when it's caught early. My prognosis is good."

Olivia nodded her approval. "What was it you always said about your prosthesis? I never quite understood that."

"I've always called it my 'trophy of grace.' My prosthesis has given me an opportunity to share God's love with so many who have asked why I'm not mad at Him for my cancer. It's a trophy of His tender mercy to me and my family."

"But, why aren't you mad at God?" Olivia seemed embarrassed by her question. "I mean, I can understand why others would ask you."

"My first bout with cancer helped my parents get back together after their divorce. Then, five years later, when a tumor in my leg showed up and resulted in the amputation, I learned the meaning of grace. I was only ten, but I was old enough to understand that God had spared me for a purpose."

Olivia thought a moment, her brow furrowed. "Pardon me, dear, but what is meant by 'grace'?"

"Grace is God's unmerited favor. We've done nothing to earn God's help. Yet He loves us with an unconditional love. He treats us as though we deserve His good gifts."

Olivia tilted her head, trying to comprehend Brianne's words. Just then, a young man appeared in the doorway. "Ready for your breathing treatment, Mrs. Hamilton?"

Brianne excused herself and gathered her things. She headed for her mom's house, where the family would spend New Year's Eve. She knew Meme, Holly, and Nana had been praying for her visit. The four generations of women would bring in the New Year praising God that Olivia was hearing His personal invitation for saving faith … before her health got any worse.

Hannah Harper rang the doorbell at her best friend Holly's house. The two embraced as though they hadn't just seen each other days before on Holly's birthday. "I've missed you *so much*," Hannah exclaimed. "You don't know how it is to be the one left behind."

"Yeah, left behind with all the friends from high school who are going to college here in Nashville. Or, those who still attend our church. Peabody College is blocks from your house. On the other hand, I had to start from scratch making friends at Georgetown."

"Of course. Tall blonde green-eyed beach boy types heading for law school. Poor thing."

"You always describe him that way." Holly led the way to her room. "You've never even met Blake."

"But I've seen dozens of pictures—hundreds, maybe." She flopped down on Holly's papasan chair. Holly stood above her, hands on hips. "Sorry." Hannah jumped up and headed for her friend's desk chair. "Thought I might get away with sitting on your throne for a change."

"Never!" Holly settled into her comfy cushion. The two talked about their Christmas presents and Christmas Day activities.

Hannah confided that Christmas now centered on her younger brother Denny, who was still at the age of being surprised by his gifts. An "oops" baby, Denny was in the sixth grade. He'd made no secret about what he wanted for Christmas. His obvious hints had resulted in several items under the tree.

Meanwhile, predictable Hannah always had a similar assortment of clothes and toiletries. Her parents, Ken and Lisa Harper, had made the special day interesting with a trip to see the festivities at the Gaylord Hotel. Hannah frowned and dropped her eyes as she recalled how different Christmas had become now that her older brother Hal was in the Marines.

Holly remembered that Hal was rarely home for Christmas. He'd been away at college before that, so his comings and goings had gotten less frequent over the years. She politely asked his sister how he was doing.

"He can't say much, since he's just finished training for his first assignment. But I miss him so much. He's my best friend—after you, of course!

Holly immediately felt embarrassed about the way she'd been treating Ty. After all, her brother was here in Nashville, across the hall, perfectly safe. Or was he? *As soon as Hannah leaves, I'm on my knees, Lord. Please take care of him.*

11

Ty wandered into the empty kitchen, calling his mother's name. He deposited his sports bag on the island and headed for the refrigerator. Seeing the note she'd left him, he read that she was spending the afternoon at the hospital with Olivia, and then on to Nana Amy's. In a way, Ty was relieved his mom wasn't home. Since the news of the spot on her lung, he hadn't quite known what to say to her. The "C" word was the bogyman in the Hamilton household. He hadn't figured out a way to demonstrate his concern without showing the fear he felt.

He grabbed a bottle of water and headed to his room. Soon, he heard his dad come through the front door. He'd parked on the driveway instead of in the garage. Maybe he was leaving again—leaving Ty to brood in the silence he preferred.

After a few minutes, Gavin knocked and entered his bedroom. "I'd give you a hug," he teased, "but I can't get through the barricade of clothes you've erected on the floor."

Ty grinned, and pushed a few things out of the way so his dad could sit on the edge of the bed. "How's Grandmother?" he asked.

"Haven't gotten there today, but according to Brianne she's some better. She sat up and talked to her for a while. The really good news is that she's showing some interest in spiritual things."

"Oh, really?"

"Yeah. I think Meme Jan is praying her into the kingdom. God seems to sit up and take notice when Meme asks something. She's a remarkable prayer warrior."

Ty looked at the floor. He'd yet to become comfortable talking about his faith, although he'd become a Christian shortly after he turned thirteen. He made a mental note to work on that.

The two shared a quick meal of leftovers before Gavin headed for the hospital. Alone again, Ty checked his social media sites and played video games. Then, a text message from Guillermo came through. Ty grabbed his car keys and left the house. He was glad to have something to do besides worrying about his mom. New Year's Eve might be more exciting than he'd thought.

Gavin's hospital visit didn't last long. His mom was restless and had a hard time focusing on his attempts at conversation. Her raspy breathing alarmed him, since she'd seemed better earlier in the day, according to Brianne. Parker would be home tomorrow. Together they'd work out a plan for where she would go when the hospital released her.

She'd offered no resistance when he'd pecked her on the cheek before leaving. Feeling somewhat guilty, he headed for Layton and Amy's house, where the New Year's Eve party was in full swing. Layton and Phil were in the man cave watching a football game. The playoff games were in sight. Relieved to have something to take his mind off his wife's and his mother's health, Gavin let out a long sigh. Maybe the Tennessee Titans would win a playoff game this year.

Parker entered his mother's hospital room early New Year's Day. He'd only been home a few hours, but with chronic insomnia, he'd learned to function with only a few hours of sleep. He hoped to be at his mother's bedside when the doctor made rounds.

Olivia turned from her breakfast tray as he approached. A slow smile appeared as she reached for his hand. He kissed her cheek and deposited a vase of flowers on the bedside table. "From Kathy's winter garden."

"Lovely," she replied. Olivia was still trying to put together days and times. "You're home from your trip, I see. How did it go?"

Parker hadn't been around to observe the change in his mother's tone. Normally, she'd have immediately steered the conversation to her situation and informed him how he was to fit in with her plans. This interest in his trip was unprecedented.

"Thanks for asking," he said. "Not as well as I'd hoped. Money for charities is hard to come by. With all the online sites asking for funding, competition is stiff."

"I'm sorry, dear … Here, take a piece of toast. I simply can't eat any more." Parker was tempted, since he hadn't stopped for breakfast. But he had more important things on his mind. "No, thanks, I'll pass."

He pulled a chair to the bed. "Mother, when you're dismissed, you'll need care. I know Louisa and Clarissa aren't due back for a week. Come to my house. Kathy begged me to ask. She's a natural-born caregiver. Loves people, loves helping out."

"No, Parker, I simply couldn't put her to that trouble. I'm sure I can find a temporary place …"

"Actually, Mother, it's not that simple. Facilities aren't geared for a week's stay. I'm afraid you're stuck with me." He reached for her hand, a pleading look in his eyes.

Taken aback, Olivia didn't have a ready response. "We'll see what the doctor says."

Parker cleared her breakfast tray and straightened her bed covers. He helped her with her hair and teeth cleaning, and she sat up in bed, pillows propped behind her.

When the doctor arrived, Parker introduced himself, and they shook hands. The doctor smiled as he turned his attention to his patient. "Mrs. Hamilton, I hear good things from the nursing staff. You're working hard at your breathing treatments, and most of the fluid is gone from your lungs. I'm planning to send you home tomorrow—that is, unless you like our food so much we can't budge you."

Olivia returned his smile, and the doctor continued, "I trust you have someone who can care for you until you have your strength back?"

"I'm that someone," Parker interjected. "She's coming home with me." Olivia tried to shake her head, but the doctor beamed his approval. He motioned for Parker to come with him as he exited. "Excuse me, Mother," Parker said. "I'll be back in a moment."

Once outside, with the door shut, the doctor's mood shifted. "Your mother's congestive heart failure won't improve. The breathing treatments will make her more comfortable, but the disease will eventually take her life. It could be a matter of years—or months." He briefly described the progression of the disease. "I'll leave detailed instructions for Mrs. Hamilton's care in my dismissal papers. When the time comes, I'll arrange for home health care."

After the doctor walked away, Parker stood in the hall a few minutes, trying to absorb the news that his mother possibly only had months or a few years ahead of her. Telling her would serve no purpose. He slipped back into the room, relieved to find that she had fallen asleep.

The following day Parker returned to take her to his house. He carried her frail form up the stairs into their guest suite without any drama. Seemingly resigned to staying with Kathy and her son for at least the following week, she hadn't put up a fight.

Ty rang the doorbell at Parker's house. He answered the door, causing Ty's heart to skip a few beats. Ty still hadn't read any of the testimonies from Parker's book. Fortunately, Parker didn't ask about it and showed him to Grandmother's room.

"Mother, see who's come to visit. Looks like he's got something for you."

Olivia was sitting on a chaise lounge with a light blanket drawn around her knees. She glanced up from her book and took in the sight of her grandson with an appraising eye. "My, you've grown! And what a handsome young man! Come closer."

Ty edged toward her, extending a coffee table book with scenes of Italy that his mother hoped Alexis and Olivia had explored together. Olivia registered surprise as she thumbed through its pages.

Ty shifted his legs from one to the other. He'd run out of excuses for not visiting her. "You're the only family member who hasn't seen her since she's been ill," his mom had pleaded. "Please. You don't have to stay long." Encouraged by this news, he'd agreed.

His plan had been to deliver the book, extend his hopes for her speedy recovery, and head home as fast as the speed limit allowed. Unlike Holly, who as a child had wanted a relationship with her grandmother, his approach had been to hide behind his mother's legs. He wished for her now.

Grandmother looked up from the book. "Lovely photos. Do thank your mother for it. … And how have you been, my dear?"

"Huh … fine." He fought for a few facts about himself. "I'm a senior, uh, doing good. In the Spanish club. I run track. That's about it."

"Do you have a girlfriend?"

"No, no, I don't." Inwardly he cursed his light complexion with its ready blush.

"Then I'm sure you've broken many hearts."

To his dismay, the blush spread. His grandmother reached for his hand, making it harder for him to dash to the door. She held his lightly in her small wrinkled one. "I'm so glad you came."

"I—I'm sorry you've been sick," he stammered. "I hope you enjoy the book." Ty backed toward the door, and waved, feeling utterly embarrassed and tongue-tied. "See you later."

Of course, he backed right into Parker, who'd been observing the scene. "Bye, Uncle Parker. See you around." With that he took off down the stairs and out the door.

Parker watched his nephew flee out the front door. He scratched his chin, elbow perched in his left hand. Slowly, he turned back to his mother. Pausing for a moment, he thought about asking her to share her impressions of the almost grown-up Ty.

Then he thought better of the idea. She had a wistful look on her face. His mother needed a little more time to get used to being around family.

Kathy had prepared a bland casserole for dinner per doctor's advice. No salt. She and Parker ate with Olivia at the round table in the guest room to give her some company. Her mother-in-law didn't complain about the meal, although she ate very little. When they were finished, Kathy scurried down the stairs and returned with Olivia's favorite herbal tea.

"Thank you, dear," Olivia responded. "This should help me rest. I've always enjoyed a cup of tea before bedtime.

Kathy said, "You're welcome. I'm sorry to rush off, but tonight is my ladies Bible study. I'll see you tomorrow morning with your breakfast tray." She pecked Olivia's cheek with a kiss and darted out the door.

Parker started to rise, but Olivia motioned for him to sit in the armchair beside her. Minutes passed while she appeared to be collecting her thoughts. "I have few regrets about my life," she began. "I've certainly had it easier than most folks. But I do wish I'd gotten to know my grandchildren."

Parker took a chance. "Why is that, Mother?"

"Why did I keep you all at arm's length, you mean?"

Parker's jaw dropped.

"I may not have a lot of time left. I've needed to get something off my chest for a long time. I guess it might as well be now." Parker prayed silently as his mother settled her blanket across her feet.

12

"When I was a little girl, I idolized my father," Olivia began. "And, I must admit, he spoiled me rotten. We had a horse farm, as you know, and Dad taught me to ride before I started first grade. I worked with him and the farm hands cleaning the stables, grooming the horses—standing on a step stool because I was so little—feeding them their dinner. I loved the horses, gave them names, played like they were brothers and sisters.

"Sometimes, when I couldn't sleep—Parker, I'm afraid your insomnia is genetic—I'd go to the barn and lay in the straw outside the stalls, comforted by my four-legged friends. Eventually, I'd get sleepy enough to go back to my bed.

"One night, when I was thirteen, I lay awake until I couldn't stand being in bed anymore. I headed for the barn, as usual, and noticed a dim light in my father's office. That seemed unusual, so I went to investigate. When I opened the door, I saw him with another woman … in a compromising position.

"I cried out and ran back to the house, where I fell sobbing onto my bed. Of course, I woke my mother—your Gram Sloan—who came into my room to see what had happened. In a few minutes, Dad came in, hair tousled, shirttail half tucked, with the most sorrowful look I've ever seen.

"I—I never forgave him. My mother did, but our family was never the same. Mother was a strong Christian, as you know. I thought, how could a loving God allow my mother to be hurt so badly? In a way, I never forgave her for not punishing Dad.

"He tried, as best he could, to make it up to us. But I'm a stubborn woman—as you know. I held on to my resentment and let it color all my relationships. I trusted no one—not even your father. As it turned out, Hollister was much too caught up in his work to entertain an affair ... and probably much too afraid of losing my inheritance. Strange, don't you think, that he lost it anyway?"

Olivia paused, leaving Parker time to reflect on the courtroom scene, when the judge had awarded Gram Sloan's inheritance to her grandson instead of his parents.

Looking through the window to some place far away, Olivia sighed. "I robbed myself of the joy I could have had as a wife and mother. I kept busy, but I was an empty shell functioning as though something lived inside me.

"My dad died shortly after my eighteenth birthday. He had a sudden heart attack and was gone before I ever had a chance to say I was sorry ... sorry for every mean word and look. Sorry I had wasted the last years I had with him. I had even turned against my mother, thinking she was weak. Many years later she also died without my forgiveness." She paused, lifting deeply troubled eyes toward him. "Parker, is it too late for me to make amends with those who are left?"

Overcome with emotion, Parker shook his head and gripped his mother's hand so hard she finally had to pull it away. "So much makes sense now," he said. "Mother, we're going to get through this. With God's help, it's never too late."

That night Parker's insomnia was friend, not foe. His wakefulness gave him time to process his mother's revelations. He wondered if he should tell Gavin or wait for Olivia to do so. For now, he liked being the only one who knew, the only one in the family to feel a special bond with his mother. He'd waited more than fifty years for a connection with her.

When Kathy got home from her Bible study, he tried to act as though it had been a normal evening. He wasn't ready to share his mother's revelations. Plus, he had no idea what her next moves might be. Would this be their secret? He simply didn't know.

The next morning he was up early for a breakfast meeting. He passed

Kathy in the foyer carrying a breakfast tray toward the stairwell. "Have a great day," she said, as he brushed her cheek with a kiss.

"You, too. Give Mother my love. I haven't seen her this morning."

"Will do."

With that he bounded down the front steps to his car, thoughts swirling around his new insights into his mother's lifelong self-isolation.

Once in Olivia's room, Kathy set the tray on the round table near the chaise lounge. She helped Olivia to the table and got her situated. "Mrs. Hamilton, would you like for me to stay or would you rather watch a morning news show?"

"Oh, please, call me Olivia. I've been meaning to tell you that. And, I believe for now, I'll just take in the sound of the birds singing outside my window. Would you mind opening the drapes for me?"

"Of course not." As she left the room, Kathy felt as though she'd had an out-of-body experience. Her mother-in-law wanting to hear birds sing? Maybe it was the angels coming to take her.

In twenty minutes she was back with fresh coffee for both of them. Olivia seemed glued to the scene outside the window. Finally, Kathy spoke. "How are you feeling today?"

"Truthfully, I find it hard to breathe well when I'm lying down. Sitting up feels much better."

"You have a breathing treatment later this morning," Kathy recalled. "That should help."

"Yes, yes, I'm sure it will." She turned her head in her daughter-in-law's direction. "I have an awkward request. Believe me, I have a reason for asking. Would you tell me again how your first husband died?"

Kathy's startled expression embarrassed the older woman. "Please don't take offense. I know it's a painful subject. But I have a question for you later."

Kathy drank a few sips of coffee before launching into the story. "My husband, Roy Collins, was a pastor, you know. He was on the planning group that got the low-income medical clinic started—the one where Parker was the medical director after—after his probation ended. I began working there during the day as the receptionist while my two older children were in school. Parker and I practically ran the place for the three years he was there.

"My son Matthew was born during that time, and Parker allowed me to bring him to the clinic while I was nursing. Parker claims he changed more diapers than I did." Kathy smiled and took another sip of coffee.

"About a year after Parker left to begin the halfway house, Roy was in his church office one Monday when the bell rang indicating someone was at the door. The secretary buzzed his office to say the caller appeared to be a street person. Roy said to let him in. The man came through the door wielding a knife and threatening to kill them unless they gave him money.

"Roy and Janet pulled out their wallets. Together they had about $55.00. The man wasn't satisfied. Seemed to think the church had money in some vault on the premises. Of course, it didn't. One of the deacons had deposited Sunday's receipts, and all checks had to be signed by the treasurer. The man became enraged and began stabbing Roy. Janet ran and hid in a storage closet. When the man left, she called 9-1-1, but by the time the paramedics arrived, Roy was dead."

Olivia nodded. "They caught the man, didn't they?"

"Yes. He's serving a life sentence. May I ask why you wanted to hear all this?"

"Have you forgiven him?"

Startled, Kathy paused. "I have. I was called to testify at his sentencing hearing. I forgave the defendant and explained that God was willing to forgive him, also, through Jesus' shed blood. I told him I hoped I would see him in heaven, and I knew Roy would welcome him there as well."

"That seems incredible to me," Olivia mused. "How could you do that?"

"Because God has forgiven me of many sins, and my sins were no easier to forgive than his. Both cost Jesus His life. He made it possible to restore our relationship with God that had been broken by sin."

"Is there a name for that?" Olivia looked sheepish. "A church word?"

"It's called *mercy*. The power to forgive. How could I accept God's gift of forgiveness for myself and deny it to my husband's killer? I pray for this man every day, hoping someday to hear he's given his life to Christ."

Olivia placed her hand atop Kathy's. "Thank you dear. You've given me much to think about."

"You're welcome." Kathy put her free hand on top of Olivia's. "You know, Parker ministered to my children and me through that horrible ordeal. I don't know how we would have gotten through it without him and the Sloan House staff and our loving church family. Thank you for your gift to me of a compassionate husband."

"I'm afraid I had little to do with that. Parker's a different person than the young man I watched grow up. Remember, I was there when they took him away to his own prison cell. He's turned his life around."

"Actually, Olivia," Kathy called her by her first name, "Someone else turned his life around. Parker would never take the credit."

"So it seems. So it seems."

13

Across town Gavin sat impatiently in the waiting room while Brianne lay quietly in a CAT scan chamber. With his open briefcase, iPad, and remains of his coffee and sandwich strewn around him, he'd erected a kind of buffer zone that would infer, "I'm a busy man; don't bother me." He didn't want company, not even family members, for his vigil. So far, feigning work had sealed his isolation.

The specialist had been very encouraging about the spot on Brianne's right lobe of her lung. Dr. Givens had determined it was a small and treatable tumor—the best possible scenario if, indeed, it was cancerous. Brianne was in good health, otherwise. He would recommend a form of treatment once the diagnosis was complete.

When Brianne emerged through the glass doors of the radiation unit, smiling and looking like a million bucks, Gavin breathed a sigh of relief. Whatever was going on, his wife was dealing with it as she always had with grace and dignity. "Shall we go home?" she winked, as though finishing a dinner date.

Gavin took her arm and led her to their parked car. Once behind the wheel, he asked, "Well?"

"I'll get a call from the doctor when all the results are in, and we'll go from there."

Amazed by her calm demeanor, Gavin probed. "Like when? When will he call?"

"I have no idea. The radiologist reads the CAT scan, and then he'll put all the information together for the doctor. I think you're going to have to put on your patience pants."

For Gavin, the next couple of days passed like a snail's race. Ty started the second semester of his senior year. Brianne and Holly went for a brief shopping trip, "just for necessities," as Holly put it. His wife took a casserole to Kathy, who was trying her best to keep Olivia comfortable. And he finished a court case that had been hanging for months.

Finally, Dr. Givens, the specialist, called. Fortunately, when the call came in the kids were in the family room fighting for control of the video world. Brianne put the phone on speaker. The news was mixed. Brianne's tumor was cancerous. The doctor paused to let the reality sink in. But the treatment plan sounded promising.

"What I'm recommending," the doctor said, "is a form of radiation therapy called stereotactic body radiotherapy." He went on to say this form of radiation aims many beams of radiation from different angles at the lung cancer and can be completed in a few treatments. "If this works, we won't need to do surgery," he concluded.

"Sign me up," Brianne practically shouted, relieved that no invasive therapy had been suggested. Then she glanced at Gavin. "Hon, is that okay with you?"

Gavin was still grappling with the big C word and couldn't take it all in. He asked the doctor, "Could you send a link to several sources? I'd like to find out more about this therapy." The doctor agreed, and the call ended. Gavin grabbed Brianne's hand, and they sat in silence.

"I know you're scared," she said, "but let's look on the bright side. I've certainly faced worse, and God has brought me through. Let's thank Him for this new form of radiation and pray that it works wonders."

As Brianne prayed, a lonely tear rolled down Gavin's cheek. Was it fear? Relief? A combination of the two? His pent-up emotions took over, and he cried through his wife's loving tribute to God's care and compassion. She took him in her arms and rocked him gently.

As promised, Dr. Givens sent Gavin several articles featuring Stereotactic Body Radiation Therapy. He made notes from the lengthy and often technical articles. Then he took his findings to share with Brianne. She was lying on the couch in her office, eyes open but looking at nothing in particular. He grabbed a throw from the end of the couch and covered her body.

"Thanks," she murmured. "And now for that cup of herbal tea?"

"Your wish, Madame." Gavin hurried to the kitchen, where he found her stash of tea bags. Minutes later, Brianne took her first sip.

"Very good." She sighed. "I think I'll just let you take over the kitchen duties for a while."

"Then we're in for a rough patch, darling." He ran his fingers through her tousled strawberry hair. "Meanwhile, I'm now the world's living expert on SBRT."

"Which is?"

"Your radiation treatment for your tumor." He looked at his notes. "First, SBRT is not an immediate cure. Radiation therapy keeps working for weeks or months after treatment ends. It begins with what is called a simulation to map out the treatment site, get the correct dose, and protect nearby healthy tissue."

"How long does that take?"

"Usually less than four hours." Gavin handed her several stapled sheets of paper. "This should tell you what to expect. Then, the radiologist schedules your treatment. It may be a single treatment. Or, more likely, three to eight treatments, usually given every other day."

"That's a relief. Some of my friends with cancer have radiation for six weeks or more."

"It's quick because your cancer was caught early and involves only one spot. Side effects are few, such as a cough or fatigue."

"Hey, I've got those already."

"You'll have checkups, of course, once the SBRT is finished. Meanwhile, this doctor," he said pointing to himself, "recommends relaxation and lots of herbal tea, at your command."

"You're a Doctor of Jurisprudence, not a *real* doctor." She grinned at his sourpuss face. "However, your treatment plan sounds good. My first command is to call my parents and tell them all you've told me. You know how concerned they are about my prognosis."

"Will do." Gavin hurried back to his home office where his medical articles lay in piles on his desk. He knew Layton would lead them in prayer—one of the best perks of marrying into the Brooks family.

Parker sat in his study looking over the foundation's financial reports. Kathy had just joined him with two cups of hot coffee. When Parker's cell tune began playing, he saw the call was from Gavin. He suspected the call would concern Brianne's health.

"Hey, bro," Gavin began. "Thanks for picking up my call. Is this a good time to talk?"

"Yes. In fact, Kathy just sat down across from me. Do you want me to put the phone on speaker, or is this another call about my embezzling money from the firm?" He winked at his wife.

Gavin chuckled. "Maybe that's a conversation for another time. Yes, please put it on speaker." His smile faded.

"What's the news?" Parker ventured.

"Bad news, good news."

Kathy clutched her husband's hand. He replied, "Say on."

"The tumor is cancerous. The good news is it's treatable."

Parker looked at Kathy as if to say, *help me out, here.* She tightened her grip on his hand. Her gaze communicated *there's hope.*

Gavin continued. "A new radiation therapy holds promise. We're checking it out."

Kathy spoke into the phone. "Brianne, Gavin, we love you," she began. "We'll continue to lift you to heaven's throne. Please know we're here for you twenty-four seven."

"Just knowing you're caring for Mother means a lot. Especially now," Gavin added.

Parker regained some of his composure. "Mother's doing well. In fact, she's making progress in ways you'd never expect. More on that later."

"Goodnight, then." Gavin clicked off the phone.

Parker turned to Kathy. "Now to tell our children."

14

In her kitchen, Kathy Hamilton wrapped a portion of what she'd cooked for their evening meal to take to Gavin and Brianne's home. As she passed Parker's study, she told him where she was going and headed out the front door to where her car was parked on the circular driveway.

Parker headed up the stairwell to spend some time with his mother. She had just finished her portion of the meal. "Those pork chops were delicious." Olivia sighed contentedly. "I'm going to have to tell Clarissa she has stiff competition. How did you find such a wonderful cook?"

"Well, we worked together for three years at the medical clinic," Parker began, unaware of her conversation with Kathy earlier in the week. "She was the receptionist when I served as the medical director. Of course, she did much more. She filed medical records, straightened the waiting room, and often served as babysitter for youngsters whose mothers were having appointments they didn't need to see or hear.

"Her husband, a local pastor, was a tremendous supporter of the clinic. After her husband Roy died, I tried my best to help her children work through their grief. When I decided to move out of The Sloan House, Kathy helped me decorate this house."

Olivia piped up, "She didn't know she was decorating her own future home."

Parker laughed. "Nor did I! Then one day she showed up alone at a Sloan Foundation fundraiser sponsored by her church. I invited her to dinner afterward—just to catch up on her children." Parker winked. "Eight months later she pushed and pulled me down the aisle."

They both laughed. He continued, "I really did—do—love her children, just as much as if they were mine. I miss them now that they're grown. But I'm so fortunate to have their mother."

Olivia inquired, "So … have you and Kathy talked about … ?"

"If you mean, did I say anything to her about our conversation, the answer is no."

"Actually, I was referring to my conversation with her."

"No. I haven't heard about one in particular."

"I asked her to tell me about Roy's death. I couldn't remember the details."

Parker took in the information with a puzzled expression. "Why would you want to? The killing was brutal and senseless."

"I wanted to know if she'd forgiven the man who stabbed her husband. I wanted to know how she did it."

"Oh." Parker paused to recover from his bout of anger. He realized his mother was still struggling with her choice not to forgive her father for his indiscretion. "So, what did she say?"

"Kathy said God had forgiven her sins, so she felt she had to forgive this murderer. I hardly see how the two can be compared."

"How did she compare them?"

"If I understand what she said, God forgives all sins if we ask. It doesn't matter if they're big or small." She paused. "When I was in the hospital, Jan Dyer and Brianne both spoke to me about God's grace—how he loves us even when we don't deserve it."

"We never deserve it, Mother. That's what's so incredible about grace. It's truly unmerited favor."

Olivia looked down. "My dad deserved a second chance. I refused to give it to him."

Parker had the good sense to pause and let her words linger. "Forgiving is hard. We resist letting go of our hurts. That's the human condition. We act out of our human nature, instead of God's nature."

"Mercy. That's His nature." Olivia let a stray tear fall onto her cheek. "How can I forgive myself? I was so ugly to him."

Parker moved to her side and wrapped his strong arms around her. "That's something you'll have to work through. I'll pray for you, Mother. We all will." Olivia buried her face in his shoulder.

Several days later Parker sat facing the rest of the family, all of whom had cleared their calendars to be present at his house. Ty and Holly took the loveseat while their parents and Kathy occupied the couch. Parker settled Olivia in the armchair beside his. A woolen throw covered her lap.

"This is actually Mother's meeting," Parker began. "I'm going to turn it over to her. But first, I'd like to lead us in a prayer." They bowed their heads. "Lord God, show Yourself to us in this place tonight. May we feel Your love in a special way. Give us understanding and compassion, and bless the one who will share her heart with us. Amen."

Parker looked at Olivia, who shifted uncomfortably in her chair. "My dears, I asked you to come tonight to hear a story, one that I hope will shed some light on my relationship with each of you." Olivia then related the experience she'd had with her father and its consequences. When she concluded, everyone sat in stunned silence.

"Since the age of thirteen, I've lived in my own self-inflicted isolation. I lost the capacity to trust. I shut myself off from anyone who could hurt me, and I'm afraid, my dears, that included all of you. I want to ask your forgiveness, although I expect it will take some time. I want to learn to love and trust again. I'm so sorry." Olivia crumpled in a wave of tears.

Each family member rose to circle her chair, murmuring words of encouragement. When most of the tears were dried, Gavin spoke. "Mother, we've always loved you, and I think I speak for everyone in offering our forgiveness. We hope to have many years to grow to love you more—to share our lives with you."

Parker winced at his knowledge that Olivia's time might be short. In his spirit, he felt his mother knew this, as well. Nevertheless, she hugged each of them in turn and thanked them for a new start.

Now, thought Parker, *if she could just have a glimpse of God's mercy for her.*

Gavin sat alone in the family room, nestled in the big recliner he had jokingly declared off-limits to other family members. Holly had not easily given up her "right" to sit in it. But she'd never grown tall enough for her feet to touch the floor. Truth was, the chair swallowed her. Grudgingly, she'd announced her dad could have the ugly old thing.

Now as he lay back against the head cushion, he felt a tremendous weight had been lifted from his shoulders. His mother's revelations gave him insight into the family dynamics that had always plagued him. Because he had been indulged as a child, he'd been slower than Parker to pick up on his parents' emotional distance. In his teenage years, Gavin had finally realized that their granting his every wish was just as much a sign of indifference as denying his needs.

He'd had everything—and nothing. He'd lacked the important things: love, affection, interest, discipline. His parents' inattention had made it easy for Gavin to fall prey to alcohol and drugs, but until now he'd not understood his raging anger—his temper that Parker had first encountered when as an adult he had sought a relationship with his younger brother. Gavin had been mad at the world for what he'd missed. And mad at Parker for finding solace in his faith.

After Gavin became a Christian, his attitude toward his parents softened. Because he'd worked in his father's law firm, he'd had an opportunity to observe the fabric of Hollister's life woven with money, prestige, and power but frayed by twisting the law to suit his purposes. Hollister lacked character and integrity. Gavin could have despised him. Instead, he came to pity him.

He'd always thought of his mother as victim. Now, she had owned her part in the emotional isolation he'd felt. Confession always brings a freeing of the soul, like fresh rain pouring from the skies. He'd meant it when he offered his mother forgiveness. And like her, he wished he could have forgiven his father before he died. The comparison stunned him.

Where's the replay button? he asked himself, aching for the father-son relationship that would never be. Now he felt even more compassion toward his mother.

With a start, he lurched forward in his chair. Soon Ty would be grown. How would his son describe their relationship?

15

When Gavin came to bed, Brianne rolled toward him. He took her in his arms and held her close. "I'm proud of you, Brianne Hamilton."

"Huh?" she asked sleepily.

"For sharing a word of grace with my mother. For bearing patiently all she's put you through all these years. For forgiving her."

Brianne laid her head on his chest. "No credit here. A divine privilege, I'd say."

"Well, I love you for it." He tenderly kissed his wife and fell asleep with her in his arms.

Holly couldn't sleep. Her mind chewed on Olivia's revelations, turning the details over and over. Truth be told, she was a little upset that she'd not been more curious about what had caused her grandmother to withhold her love. Normally, she'd have pieced together what she'd known of her grandmother's story and sought to find answers.

Holly should have guessed a hidden chapter could be found in the book of Olivia Sloan Hamilton's life. Now that she knew the dark mystery, her heart melted with sorrow for all her grandmother had suffered. Meme had said God was up to something. Her words were coming true.

A sudden realization caused Holly to sit up in bed. She whispered excitedly. "And I got to be home when all of this happened! If I'd been in DC, I'd have missed one of the most important times in my family's history. And to see God at work in a person's life! It doesn't get any better than this." Holly's praises finally escorted her into a deep and restful sleep.

Ty tossed and turned. He didn't much like family drama, tears, kisses, and hugs. Yeah, he was glad for Grandmother Olivia to get stuff off her chest, but by the time the family got home, he'd felt suffocated by another Hamilton feel good story of forgiveness and grace.

Why can't we be a normal family? he asked himself for the thousandth time. Instead, he'd been dropped into one filled with villains and heroes, good and evil, God versus the powers of darkness. Love conquers all. The good guys always come out on top.

Which am I? he wondered.

"God Almighty be praised," Meme shouted, her hands lifted toward heaven. The Brooks and Dyers sat in their living room relishing Gavin's retelling of Olivia's story. He'd let them know that Olivia had given her permission. She had owned her sorrow over missed relationships. She also wanted Meme to know how important a role she had played in her decision to ask for forgiveness.

"Oh, you just wait," Meme waved a finger in the air. "We're praying for another miracle, the miracle of salvation.

Papa Phil threw a protective arm across his wife's shoulders. "Olivia might just as well give up the fight."

Gavin spoke up. "While we're praying for miracles, let's remember my precious wife as she battles cancer again." Heads nodded.

"And I've got another request." He leaned in, elbows on knees. "I'm concerned about Ty, as you know. When he found out the agenda for yesterday's family meeting, he didn't want to be there. I know he's a teenage guy. He's still learning what to do with his feelings. And he's not dealing well with his mother's illness. God knows I try not to worry about him but …"

Everyone nodded his and her understanding. Amy squeezed her eyelids together and reached for Layton's hand.

Zack Bryson settled into his squeaking chair and placed his elbows on the old maple desk. Its polished surface spoke of days gone by when it probably sat in a principal's office. Now stuffed into his makeshift office at Meadville High School, the desk looked as decrepit as the scuffed floor and nicked walls.

He certainly hadn't become a school security officer for the glamour. Zack stared at the stack of files facing him, wondering which to pick first. Classes had just started back from the holidays, and for the moment all the students appeared to be out of the halls and into classrooms.

He glanced at the monitors above the doorway. His partner, Fred Larsen, was just entering the empty cafeteria and checking exterior doors. The men varied the daily patrols so as not to be predictable to anyone who wanted to cause trouble.

Meadville was a large urban school with the usual socio-economic mix, ethnic cliques, and some gang activity, but it had an even larger population of really good kids who tried hard and just wanted a decent education. Same as most schools.

Along with pranks, bullying, and fights, he faced the ongoing fear of gun violence. Adrenalin pumped through his veins from the moment his shift began until it ended. Would today be the day? He had to think that way, go over the drills in his mind, stay alert. Someone's life might depend on it.

Heroin was a growing problem, with two overdose deaths since September. Mostly, he dealt with marijuana, cocaine, and meth. Some new combination always hovered over the illegal drug trade and made its way into the juvenile population.

The new dress code helped a lot with gang activity, but the big difference was Vince Merrill. Dr. Merrill had his back, no doubt about it. The principal's large frame didn't hurt, either. No one missed the 6'7" head towering above the students coming and going in the locker areas.

Zack picked up a folder, opened it, and settled back in his chair to analyze its contents. A knock on the door startled him. He glanced at his cell phone calendar to see if he should be expecting anyone. No, no appointments.

"Come in."

"Hey, Sgt. Bryson, how's it going?" The lanky figure dropped into the only chair facing his desk.

"Hey, yourself. Do you have a hall pass?"

"Sure."

Zack took the outstretched form, glanced at it, signed it, and handed it back. He placed his fingers together and sat looking at the young man in front of him. After a lengthy pause, he said, "It's too dangerous. I can't risk putting you in that kind of situation. In fact, I won't risk it."

"You can't stop me. Not unless you have me tailed or lock me up. And I haven't exactly done anything yet."

Zack shot him an exasperated look.

The young man leaned in, elbows on knees. "You said the cops—I mean, the police—have been on his trail for months."

"Only told you that so you'd know we have it under control. We don't need your help."

"Fine. But you're not the one seeing the damage up close and personal. To you it's a case. To me, it's my classmates."

"You don't think I care?" A red streak inched up the sergeant's neckline. "Timing is everything on these drug deals. We have to have evidence—hard evidence that will stand up in a court of law. No second-hand information, no 'a friend told me …'"

"I can do that! Provide the evidence, I mean. I'm the bait. I set the trap. All you have to do is show up."

"Just in time to keep him—or more likely, them—from blowing your brains out? And ours, too, for that matter. Me? I'm paid to do this. You're a senior, months from graduating, with a clean record and a bright future. Let me do my job."

Now Zack was standing, hands on desk. His angry gaze followed the figure out the door. "Use your brain kid!" He sank back into his chair. Not this guy or any other student at Meadville High was a match for Augusto Villarreal.

16

Holly couldn't resist showing up for lunch at her old high school, where she'd been a popular student a semester ago. Ty would be embarrassed and try to ignore her, but he'd appreciate the gesture. She was determined to show him he was more than a little brother to her. Ty seemed to relish the role of left-out family member, although he'd assigned the role to himself.

When Ty came through the cafeteria line and saw her standing in front of him, he did a double take. Holly led him to a table where the sack lunch she'd packed for herself was sitting. Ty motioned for the young man behind him to join them.

He introduced Guillermo as a friend he'd met in math class. Guillermo greeted her warmly. "¿Señorita, como usted esta? I've heard a lot about you."

"Oh, really?" Holly exclaimed. "I hope some of it was good."

Guillermo grinned, and the three began eating. Holly asked, "Are you the friend Ty exchanged Christmas presents with?"

Guillermo gave Ty a puzzled glance. "Must've been some other good-looking guy." Ty shrugged and looked away.

Uh-oh. I've put my foot in it this time, Holly realized. Ty would give her a piece of his mind when they got home.

"I just jumped to the wrong conclusion," she retorted. Holly, seated on Ty's bed, folded her defiant arms across her chest. "Get over it."

"I'm over it. You get over it." Ty sighed and moved to his desk across the room. "Forget the whole thing."

"I liked Guillermo," she continued, paying no attention to her brother's request. "He seems very nice. Why don't you invite him over sometime?"

"I will … after—I mean, soon."

Ty's confusing response raised her detective instincts to high alert. But the look on his face clearly read, "Discussion over." That was OK with Holly. She'd figured out other mysteries with less to go on. Ty had never been clever enough to stop her.

In her bed, Holly fumed after another tedious conversation with Blake, who had no news because he sat in his bedroom and moped about being alone. Holly called her best friend.

Hannah answered on the first ring.

"Hey, girlfriend," Holly began. "Do you remember a kid named Guillermo Sanchez from Meadville High?"

"I'm thinking," Hannah replied. "And hello to you, too."

"Oh, sorry," Holly responded. "I'm on a case."

Hannah knew all about Holly's fascination with sleuthing, so she didn't even ask for a reason. "Just a minute. I'll pull out our yearbook. How's he classified?"

"Junior last year—nice looking, seems smart. A friend of Ty's."

"And you're asking me? Hang on … here he is. Oh, yeah, I had choir with him. Great baritone."

"So what'da'ya know about him?"

"Clean fingernails. I like that in a guy."

"Cute."

Hannah kept searching. "He was in the Spanish club … figures …oh, look, he's standing next to Ty in the club photo. Apparently, they are friends."

Holly sighed. "Thanks. I'll keep you posted. See you tomorrow for lunch." She clicked off her Web search. *I guess I'm overreacting again,* she concluded. *What a shame. I was hoping at least for a police record.* She pouted as she pulled up her covers and turned off the bedside lamp.

By Friday night Gavin was exhausted. He'd not expected Meme Jan and Papa Phil for dinner, although he enjoyed their company. He'd waved goodbye and ambled into the family room, shedding one shoe and then the other before settling into his recliner.

Holly had driven the Dyers home and planned to stay awhile at Nana and Grandpa's. Ty stopped in to say he was going out and left in somewhat of a hurry. Within minutes, Gavin was sound asleep. When he awoke, the room was dark except for a little slit of light showing beneath the door to Brianne's office.

He'd barely gotten his bearings when his cell tune began playing. "Good evening," he answered in his most professional voice. Surely, a client wouldn't be calling this late on a Friday night. Within a minute he was retrieving his shoes and heading toward the mud room to find his jacket. Brianne poked her head out of her office. He turned to face her, eerily pale and trembling. "I've got to go. That was the captain at the south police precinct. Tyler is being questioned on a possible drug charge."

Gavin knew he was speeding, but he didn't care. A few more blocks … *God, tell me what to do! … What to say? … God, I want to be there for Tyler. Help me keep my temper in check. Give me courage to face this … this … whatever it is. Lord, I feel so helpless.*

Tears washed his face. He felt sick to his stomach. As a light changed to red, he stomped on the brakes, pounding the steering wheel in frustration. At the police station Gavin pulled into the first available parking spot. He jumped from the car and dashed for the door. Inside, he looked around, not sure what to do next. An officer at the information window motioned him over.

"Gavin Hamilton … my son Tyler is being held here?"

"Yes, sir. I'll get the captain."

Gavin had known Captain Perez for years. Their paths crossed often in the courthouse, and although Gavin never handled criminal cases, he made it a point to know most everyone he passed. In a minute he saw him come through a metal door and smile wanly in his direction.

Captain Perez extended a hand while running his other one through a mass of curly black hair. "Mr. Hamilton, I don't know what we've got here. A bunch of guys are in the holding cell while we try to get this sorted out. I recognized your son's name from the information we gathered about him when we interviewed him. Do you by chance know a young man named Guillermo Sanchez?"

"No, no, I don't believe so."

"He and Tyler say they're friends."

Gavin slumped back against the wall. What else did he not know about his son?

Just then another officer came through the front door, also in a hurry and also looking for Captain Perez. The two shook hands. "Congratulations on the sting, Capt. Perez. Looks like you got the gang leaders this time."

"I'll have to see Villarreal in court before I believe it. … Oh, Sgt. Bryson, this is Gavin Hamilton. His son Tyler is …" he motioned, "back there."

"Tyler Hamilton?" Bryson furrowed his brow. "You've got to be kidding!" He headed to the metal door. "Excuse me," he said as he entered the code.

"Who's he?" Gavin demanded.

"Zack Bryson. The chief security officer at Meadville High School." Perez heard his name called and turned toward the officer at the information window.

Gavin slumped further down the wall, hands over his face, despair in the pit of his soul. His legs felt like jelly. Why was a security officer so familiar with Ty and so obviously concerned that he was in custody? He sat on the floor filled with recriminations, heaping guilt on guilt until he grew sick of himself. Somehow, he'd just expected Ty to get through adolescence without having to run interference. "Let sleeping dogs lie," as the saying went. Well, look where those sleeping dogs had gotten him.

He stood to his feet, wobbly at first, and walked to a chair facing the metal door. Behind it, Ty was locked away, no doubt scared out of his mind. And the last person he probably wanted to see was his dad.

He needed to call home, although he had nothing to report. Brianne would be beside herself with worry. He punched in his code and soon had her on the line. "Bri, I really don't know any more than when I left. Ty is in a holding cell along with some other guys. Apparently, a drug sting happened somewhere, and Ty got picked up. … I don't know. They can hold him for 24 hours without charging him. … Yes, I'll post bail. Wait at home until I can talk to him. Keep praying."

17

Just as Gavin clicked off the phone, another officer passed by, followed by a petite brunette. They were headed toward an interrogation room when Gavin shouted, "Brianne, what are you doing here?"

"Oh, hi Dad." She breezed by with a decidedly smug look on her face. "I'm an informant. Isn't that right, Sgt. Mitchell?"

The sergeant warily whisked her away before her father could stammer a response. Just then, Sgt. Bryson came through the metal door and motioned for him. Once inside the jail they turned left and walked down a narrow concrete hallway.

"What's my daughter doing here?" he demanded.

"You'll find out soon enough." They entered a small room barely large enough for four chairs and a table.

Gavin spotted Ty sitting at the table beside a Latino youth. Unlike Ty, the young man seemed pleased with himself and raised a forefinger as if in salute. Bryson motioned for Gavin to sit next to the wall opposite Ty.

Gavin repressed the urge to run to Ty's side and embrace him. Instead, he followed the protocol while Bryson took the last chair. Bryson began, "Mr. Hamilton, I regret this situation. Your son and his friend are very stubborn people. I warned them something like this would happen."

"Like what?" Gavin glowered. "Will someone tell me what's going on?"

"Dad, I ..."

"Ty, I think I'd better explain." The sergeant opened a folder in front of him.

❧

Two hours later Ty sat at the kitchen counter downing a sandwich as though it were his last meal. He swallowed the last crumbs with a gulp of milk. Holly sat across from him, with the same smug face firmly affixed. His mom busied herself with cleanup.

Holly broke the silence. "So, I guess we're supposed to call you Clark Kent, crime stopper disguised as a mild-mannered high school student." She laughed at her joke. As usual, Ty kept quiet, his head down.

"Holly, give him a break." Gavin put a protective arm around his son's shoulder. "We'll deal with this tomorrow. We're exhausted."

Brianne leaned over her son's chair. "Ty, just tell me one more time what happened. I'm still trying to put this together."

Ty gave the briefest report possible. "My friend Guillermo doesn't live in the safest part of town. He hates the gangs and drug dealing that happen on his street. We talk about it a lot.

"I decided we needed to *do* something. I talked to Sgt. Bryson at school several times. I told him we could help him pull off a drug sting and catch the bad guys. He nixed the idea. Told us to stay out of it. Said the police had it under control.

"Guillermo heard about a big drug deal coming down. Augusto Villarreal, a punk kid at Meadville who thinks he's El Chapo, was expecting a big haul. Guillermo and I followed Augusto to the pick-up place."

"Oh, no!" His mom put her hands to her face.

"That's where I come in," Holly interrupted. "On my way home from the Brooks, I saw Tyler's car coming toward me. He had his head in his music and didn't see me. So, I turned around and followed him."

"And by the way, why was that?"

"Shush, Ty. I'm getting to that."

"Since I was driving Mom's car, I don't think he noticed me. I slowed down when he pulled over to pick up someone on a curb. By then, it was getting toward dusk, and I couldn't see who it was."

"It was Guillermo."

"Obviously. Then Ty goes to a rather seedy part of town …"

"I can't believe I'm hearing this. Both my kids …," Brianne buried her head in her hands.

"So, they get out of the car and go hide in some bushes."

"Apparently, we didn't hide very well. We got picked up with the rest of Augusto's gang in the police sweep."

"That's where I come in. I called the police," Holly said, with great bravado.

"We were going to call when we had them on video," Ty sulked. "Fortunately, the sting was in progress when the cops showed up." Turning to his sister, he retorted. "You almost messed up the whole thing."

"Listen to him," she railed back at him. "I probably saved your life."

"No way. We weren't in any danger."

"Hey, I backed up your story. The police believed me."

Gavin had had more than enough of his children's bickering. By now, Brianne was breathing normally and somewhat composed. He resumed the story.

"Sgt. Bryson heard about the sting and came to the station. He found out about Ty and Guillermo's role in it and chewed them out. Then I came in and got them released. Guillermo is over-the-moon happy, and Ty's probably grounded for the rest of his life. Holly, I'll hear the rest of your explanation in the morning, and it better be good. I'm going to bed now."

Ty gathered the last of his meal's trash, threw it away, and headed for his room. As he turned the corner, he saw Holly's expression. *Serves her right*, he mumbled to himself. If he weren't so wasted, he'd laugh at her all the way to his room.

Ty got up the next morning and headed for school, only to find out when he got there that he and Guillermo had been suspended for three days. Guillermo headed for the coffee shop to see if his boss would work him a few hours. Ty drove home, not sure what to do with himself.

His mom cried and called his dad, who told him to stay put. A few minutes later he called back on Ty's cell. "I've got a full court day, Ty, and no way to change my schedule. Your Uncle Parker is coming over to talk to you."

"Uncle Parker?" That was the worse news of the morning. "But why?"

"Because I can't be there and someone needs to get to the bottom of this. Parker's home for a few days with a break in his schedule. He loves you, Ty. We all do. Open up, son. I'll call your principal later today."

"You don't have to … " The phone clicked off. Ty considered an escape plan. His car was parked in the driveway. But where would he go? No place to hide. He stomped to his bedroom, slammed the door shut, and threw himself on his bed.

Half an hour later he heard the doorbell and Parker's booming voice. Quickly, he sat up and pretended to play a video game. Parker knocked, and when there was no answer, entered the room. He looked for a clear place to sit, and finding none, settled on the floor with his size 14 shoes pointed toward the ceiling.

When he didn't say anything, Ty glanced his way. His uncle sat with arms crossed leaning against the wall, staring at nothing in particular. Ty figured he could outlast him if it was a contest of wills. But why bother? Eventually, he'd have to talk.

"What do you know?" Ty asked.

"The basics."

"So, what now?"

"Your dad is concerned. This isn't like you. He wants to know if there's anything else he doesn't know about your friends and your activities. I'd say he's scared, Ty."

"Scared?" The idea that his powerful father, whose piercing dark eyes could cut through a chunk of ice, could ever be scared had never crossed his mind.

"Scared in a way you'll never know until you're a parent yourself," Parker continued. "Scared of losing you, of never having another chance to really get to know you, to show you how much he loves you."

"I never meant to scare my family." Ty rubbed his neck and considered the implications. "As soon as we had the video, we were going to call the cops. If we hadn't stayed around to see how the sting turned out, we'd never have been caught in the neighborhood. Not exactly a smart thing to do."

"And then what? Did you think the cops wouldn't trace your call? That you might not be charged as an accessory to a crime? That Sgt. Bryson wouldn't care that you'd disobeyed his orders?"

"I told him we could get Augusto. And we did. That bum's off the street, and I'm getting the riot act." His volume got louder. "What's wrong with this picture?" Ty had never spoken to his uncle in this way, but the seething anger he'd long felt toward him was bursting loose.

Parker had a quick comeback. "You get picked up and interrogated by the police … and you're mad at us? Your dad's very disappointed in you."

Bewildered, Ty finally made eye contact. "Why would he be disappointed? I thought he'd be proud … " Ty halted, having given away too much information.

Parker furrowed his brow. Pieces of the puzzle began fitting together. He ran his fingers through his short brown hair. "I think I get it."

"No, you don't!" Ty climbed off the bed and began pacing the room, kicking at random bits of clothing. "You don't know what it's like to live in this family!" He knew he should shut up. These feelings were too raw—too untamed—to be shared, especially with his uncle. But the proverbial cat was out of the bag. The words tumbled from his lips.

"What if you had a perfect family, with a perfect life, and a perfect sister everyone compared you to? And what if your uncle was this big shot celebrity who went around giving talks and writing books about how he'd overcome every obstacle in life—and you can, too?

"But I'm not perfect, and I've never done one single thing anyone can be proud of. And I can't think of clever things to say, and I'm not six feet four inches with muscles the size of tire wheels and a tearjerker story. And then I finally do something brave—something to make a positive difference in the world—and I get suspended from school and told I'm a disappointment." Ty picked up the nearest thing at hand, a drink coaster off his desk, and hurled it across the room where it hit the wall with a thud.

He sank into the desk chair and buried his head in his hands. Part of him wanted to cry, but he held the torrent in check. Mostly, he just wanted to disappear into the floor and never have to face his family again. He'd pretty much proved he'd never do anything to earn their respect.

18

Holly awoke to the sounds of male voices coming from Ty's room. She heard a door close and footsteps moving away toward the kitchen. Then Ty's music blasted her out of bed. She looked at the time: nine o'clock. Why wasn't Ty at school? Memories of last night's family drama jolted her into wakefulness.

Holly grabbed her robe and pounded on Ty's door. The music softened, but Ty didn't answer. Being Holly, she pushed open the door. Ty lay curled on his bed, tears staining both cheeks. He turned his head away from her toward the wall.

She backed away to the door. "I'm sorry ... I didn't mean to ..."

Back in her room, Holly fell to her knees. "Whatever has happened, Lord, you've got this covered by your blood. I pray for protection for my little brother, and Lord, give him wisdom as he deals with this ... this ... ." She had no idea what had just happened, who'd been in his room. And for one of the first times in her life, she felt helpless to know what to do about it.

When Parker came around the corner and encountered Brianne in the kitchen, he hastily explained that he and Ty had talked, and now he needed to process what he'd learned. He promised to get back with Gavin later in the day and asked her to give Ty some alone time. As he headed for the door, he looked back at his frightened and confused sister-in-law. "He's going to be OK," Parker asserted. "You're all going to be OK."

Parker drove aimlessly through the neighborhoods near Gavin's home. Finding himself on Belle Meade Boulevard, he turned into the entrance to Percy Warner Park. He maneuvered his car into a parking space and climbed the stone steps leading to the overlook. He sat on the top step, resting his chin on his fists.

So many memories tumbled through his mind, each sparking a new insight into his nephew. Events he'd experienced as a young man around Ty's age—those same feelings of inadequacy. In Parker's case, he added outrage at his parents' relentless pursuit of perfection, his vain attempts to gain his father's attention and approval, and his mother's cool indifference.

One incident stuck out above the others. At age 18, he'd invited his dad to be present for the senior awards ceremony at school. "I'm going to receive an award," he announced.

"And what award would that be?" Hollister asked.

"A citizenship award," he'd answered proudly.

"And what is that for?"

Caught off guard, he'd replied. "I guess for good citizenship."

"That's a rather broad category. Can you be more specific?"

"I don't know… I didn't ask for details."

"Did you do something in particular to earn this award, son?"

"Not that I know of … maybe Boy Scouts or community service projects?"

"Well, if you don't know what the award means, and you don't know what it's for, I hardly think I should rearrange my schedule to attend."

And he hadn't.

Hunger finally drove Ty from his room. Although it was mid-afternoon, Holly sat at the breakfast table in her pj's and robe drinking hot tea. His mom sat across from her. When she saw her son, she jumped up and headed for the refrigerator.

"Ty, I made you a sandwich. How about some milk to go with it?"

"Sure, thanks."

Not wanting to deal with his sister, Ty pulled out a bar stool at the kitchen island. After receiving his food, he munched silently, aware of two sets of eyes locked on his every move. *Uncomfortable* hardly described his feelings. He nibbled at the celery and carrot sticks, trying to think of something to say. Finally, the pressure got to him.

"Thanks, Mom. I'm going out for a run." He threw the wrapper in the trash and put his glass in the sink. "See y'all later." With that, he shut the back door and headed toward the familiar path through the woods.

"He didn't even speak to me," Holly wailed. "This whole situation is so bizarre!"

"Uncle Parker suggested we give him some time. He said we'd all be OK." Her mom rose from her seat and took their cups to the sink. She busied herself loading the dishwasher.

"But my heart is breaking," Holly sobbed. "I want to run after him and give him a big hug." She pursed her lips. "And then I want to jump him for causing you and Dad so much distress last night."

"As if you didn't cause any, yourself?" Holly winced.

"You know, Holly, waiting isn't your strong suit. Let's hear from your father before you take matters into your own hands. Ty's being suspended may be the worst of it. Surely, he's learned a lesson."

She shrugged. "You're probably right." She stood up and wrapped her arms around her mom's waist. "Do you think I should get dressed or just wait for bedtime?" The two women laughed as Holly headed for her room. "Love you, Mom."

"Love you to the moon and back."

Humbled by her mother's words, Holly walked back to her room. She thought about getting dressed. *I'll call Hannah. She can always cheer me up.* Holly found her phone under the pile of clothes she'd worn last night. When Hannah picked up the call, Holly plunged right in.

"I was at the police station last night, but I'm not sorry for what I did, and Ty is in BIG trouble. I possibly saved his life, but he won't even speak to me. I feel terrible."

Hannah, having been in this situation many times in the past, let Holly ramble on until she pieced the story together. When Holly finally ran out of steam, she hiccupped, a sure sign tears would follow.

"I have a younger brother too," Hannah began. "Sometimes I want to wring his neck. At the same time, I want to hug him. Let him know just how much I care. Even if he's mad at me." She paused to collect her thoughts. "Families go through rough times. People who love each other don't stay mad at each other forever. God always finds a way to bring us back together. Let Him guide your next steps."

Holly sniffed a few times, then blew her nose. "Mom says I need to be more patient."

"Ya think?"

"Vince Merrill, please." Gavin waited for the school secretary to connect him with the principal. He pulled off his tie, grateful that he was out of the judge's chambers and back in his office.

"Dr. Merrill, thank you for taking my call. Sir, I wanted to apologize for my son's behavior. Ty … Tyler Hamilton. The drug sting last night? He's been suspended for three days."

"Oh, yes, I appreciate your call. I've been apprised of the situation." Gavin could hear his squeaky chair in the background. "I assure you Ty's absence will not be unduly punitive. Classes have just resumed from the holidays. He'll not miss any important quizzes or papers, if that's what you're concerned about."

"Actually, I'm just more embarrassed than anything." Gavin cleared his throat. "We've never had to deal with this kind of problem in our family before … I had no idea … it's not how we reared Tyler, I assure you."

"I remember his sister, Mr. Hamilton. Holly was a delight. And until now, Tyler has given us no cause for alarm. I understand your concern." The principal paused. "I spoke with Sgt. Bryson this morning before the suspension. We need our students to respect our security officers and their instructions. We simply couldn't let them think that what Ty and Guillermo did was acceptable. They disobeyed orders.

"On the other hand, their hearts were in the right place, even if their heads misled them. Please don't misunderstand me ... they should have never put themselves in that situation ... but I admire their courage. Drugs are my fiercest enemy here. Don't be too hard on Ty. A little more maturity and that young man will make you proud."

After the call, Gavin clicked off the phone and sat gazing out the window on downtown Nashville. Courageous? He'd not thought of his son's actions in that way. Maybe he needed to hit the pause button before deciding on Ty's punishment.

19

Parker knocked on Gavin's office door before peeking in. "Looks like you're packing it up for the day. Let's grab a cup of java. I need to fill you in on what happened between Ty and me."

Gavin frowned, not sure he could take any more discomfort in one day. Being in court didn't seem so tough anymore. Feelings … they were tougher.

When the two men sat facing each other, hot coffee cups in hand, Parker recounted his conversation with Ty, putting the best face on his nephew's reactions. "I identify with Ty's emotions. I never measured up to Father's expectations. I grew up with a lot of insecurity about my self-worth. In Ty's case, he feels he hasn't measured up to his own expectations, and he's transferred those feelings to the rest of the family. Let's face it—we're all overachievers. It's just not Ty's style."

"Does he think I'm not proud of him? What have I done to make him feel that way?"

"It's not you, or me, or Brianne, or Holly, or anyone else in the family. He's the one who's doubted his ability to fit in, or more importantly, to make his own contribution to fighting drug addiction." Parker motioned to the waitress for a refill.

"Bro, I never earned my father's approval, no matter what I did. And he died before I ever heard him say, 'Son, I'm proud of you.' I'm glad I learned to put my self-esteem in the hands of my heavenly Father. But Ty can have both—approval from his earthly and heavenly fathers. He's lost his way trying to be someone he's not."

"You should have been a lawyer," Gavin teased.

"Father thought so, too." Parker took a long sip of his drink. "But Ty didn't pull off this drug bust simply to impress us. I'm sure, in the back of his mind, he was showing us that he, too, could fight drugs— the only way he knew. And we'd praise him for being on the team. Except we didn't—or haven't. And now, he's feeling even more alone and inadequate."

Gavin loosened his tie. "I've got a lot to think about."

The two men finished their drinks in silence.

As they stood to leave, Parker reminded Gavin that soon their mother would be transported to her own home, where Clarissa and Louisa would hover over her like clucking hens.

And Ty would spend his second day of suspension.

Ty had been afraid to call Guillermo. What had his family's reaction been? Instead, Guillermo called him first. When Ty's phone rang, he saw the familiar name on caller ID and felt both relief and anxiety. What if his best friend was mad at him too?

Instead, Guillermo was in a festive mood. His boss at the coffee shop was letting him work extra hours. He'd also picked up some extra work with his father, a construction worker. "Hey, a few more pesos never hurt," he joked. "I'll add them to my college fund."

"You mean, your parents aren't mad at you?"

"Mad? Are you loco? They're so relieved that the gang activity and drug mules have moved on to another place. At least for now. What about you?"

"My sister almost ruined the whole operation by calling the cops while we were still videotaping the drug bust. My dad is furious we wound up in jail, and my mom was frightened out of her wits. And then my uncle had to come around and tell me his sob story about growing up without his father's approval. Like I haven't heard that story before."

"I'm sorry, man. Who knew they'd react that way? I'm practically a hero in my neighborhood. What can I do?"

"Nothing. As my grandmother Nana would say, they're letting me "stew in my juices," whatever that means. My uncle wants to meet with me again this afternoon. I think my dad has turned me over to Superman."

"From all I've heard, Parker is a great guy. Maybe he's got something to say worth hearing."

"Maybe."

❧

Ty had just cleaned up after his run when he heard the doorbell. Sure enough, Superman had changed into mild-mannered Clark Kent and was standing in the living room talking to his mom. She was catching him up on her medical procedures. When she saw Ty, she turned to him. "Parker wants to take you for a drive. Isn't that nice of him?"

Feeling he had no choice, Ty nodded and grabbed his jacket. He headed out the front door, Parker following behind. Parker waved to Brianne and wished her well.

They climbed into Parker's truck and headed off to heaven only knew where. They rode in silence until Ty recognized the entrance to the Natchez Trace Parkway. He could deal with silence. He'd just settled back into the passenger seat, when Parker broke the silence.

"When we talked yesterday, I got carried away in telling about how my father never let me feel accepted for who I am. That's not your situation at all. I'm sorry if I made it sound that way." He looked over at Ty for a response.

"It's OK. I know Dad loves me."

"I think the comparison I tried to make had to do with your not feeling accepted by him. Maybe that you hadn't lived up to his expectations."

Ty thought about his response. "It's not Dad's fault. I've put the pressure on me to do something important. To make a contribution. To be a stand-out kid. But …"

"But what?" Parker's gentle tone encouraged his nephew to go deeper.

"I'm not like my superstar sister or my outgoing parents. I'm shy. I'm quiet. I think about things instead of talking about them."

"Nothing wrong with that." Parker pulled the truck off the road into an overlook parking lot. In the spring the scene would feature majestic trees and pastureland, a landscape painter's dream. Now the land lay quiet, almost desolate. He turned off the motor.

"Ty, what gets you up in the morning? What's your passion? What do you enjoy doing with your free time?"

Ty tilted his head. "Music. My alarm wakes me to my favorite radio station playing my favorite songs. I play the radio in my car. I go to bed listening to music." Ty seemed transported to a private space with no one listening. "Songs help me notice my feelings and put names to them. When I sing along, I say words I'd probably never really say to anyone. I feel heard."

Parker nodded. "I noticed a guitar in your closet when I was in your bedroom yesterday."

"Yeah. Last year's Christmas present."

"Do you play? Have you taken lessons?"

"Naw. I pick at tunes. I've taught myself how to chord. I probably should take lessons."

Parker studied the young man's face. "You come alive when you talk about your music. Your whole face changes. I think you've found your passion."

Ty looked startled, as though the idea had never occurred to him.

"The way a person stands out from the crowd," Parker continued, "is by being the person God created him or her to be. Not by trying to be like someone else."

Ty took in what Parker was saying, but he wasn't ready to commit to his uncle's insight. Could he find his voice through music? He'd have to let the idea simmer.

Parker put the truck in reverse and turned back the way they'd come. The two rode in silence for a while. Then Parker pointed to the radio. "Find me a good station," he said. Soon the two were singing along with a country band.

"You have a good voice to go along with your music." Parker's praise resulted in the familiar blush that always crept up Ty's neck and face at the wrong time.

When the truck pulled in to Ty's driveway, he got out and waved goodbye to his uncle.

20

Olivia settled onto her bed, so delighted to be back home she could barely stand it. Clarissa plumped the pillow to her mistress's specifications. Louisa unpacked the items in the suitcase and laid out a clean nightgown. "I'll draw your bathwater when you've rested from the trip home," she announced in her usual efficiency.

"And I'll make the best chicken soup you ever tasted," Clarissa declared as they withdrew from the room. Alone at last, Olivia closed her eyes and began to doze. In her dream, her father and mother were motioning her toward them. They appeared to be in their early '40s. Her mother's snow-white curls were dark again. Both wore a broad smile.

Gone were Olivia's self-doubts and recriminations. She felt immensely loved by them. She rushed into their arms. They sat together on a carpet of green grass, surrounded by lush vegetation, a rippling stream, and a vast pastureland filled with horses of every size and color. This must be heaven, Olivia thought.

A rider on a Palomino approached. He dismounted and came toward her. "Welcome, loved one." He helped her to her feet and hoisted her onto a dappled grey that whinnied her hello. It had been years since she'd ridden barebacked. The two riders took off together toward the sunset, her parents waving in the foreground of her mental picture.

"Who are you?" Olivia asked the stranger.

"I'm Jesus." He pulled a twig from between his teeth. "I've been trotting behind you for many years. Thought I'd catch up with you."

"Or maybe I slowed down to let you," she grinned.

The absurdity of her having a conversation with Jesus almost woke Olivia from her dream, but she nestled back into it, eager to talk with Him some more.

Now the two horsemen ambled into a meadow, where the horses stopped to eat grass. The abundance of pastureland impressed the former Kentucky native, who thought she could almost see a blue-green cast to the fields.

"I've loved you with an everlasting love," Jesus told her.

"I don't know how to love anymore." Olivia hung her head.

"My love is sufficient."

She looked into his eyes. Were they shining on her, or simply reflecting the setting sun? Either way, she basked in their warmth. She'd seen a glimpse of His mercy.

Olivia awoke with the most pleasurable feeling she'd had in a long time. Her breathing seemed better than usual. A smile spread across her lips as she remembered her dream—her easy conversation with Jesus, the brilliance of his eyes, the warmth of his love. Most of all, she cherished His offer of forgiveness. She felt clean inside. The hollowed-out portions of her heart were being filled with a strange substance—love.

How could a dream convince her of the reality of the unseen? It made no earthly sense.

She pressed her cell phone and waited for Louisa's voice. A warm bath would help collect her thoughts. She had a great deal to think about.

The invitation to dine at the Hamilton estate had come as a surprise to everyone—the Dyers, the Brooks, both sons and their families. Louisa and Clarissa had not prepared for a dinner party since Hollister's death. A team of housecleaners and kitchen help had been called in for the occasion. Clarissa spoke for all of them: "I sure do hope Mrs. Hamilton's health holds up to all of this."

The preparations for the evening had gone off without a hitch. A radiant hostess sat enthroned at the head of the expansive table overseeing a sumptuous dinner. Parker, seated to her right, spoke to her softly. "Mother, I'm afraid you are looking a little peaked."

Gavin, on her left, gave her an appreciative smile. "It's been a great occasion, but perhaps you should call it a night."

"Not before I've spoken," she resisted. "Please call for everyone's attention."

After the room quieted, Olivia raised her glass. Everyone followed suit. "A toast to my Lord and Savior, Jesus Christ." She clicked glasses with her astonished sons as a gasp went through the stunned group before her. She had definitely gotten their attention!

"I suppose I've always had a flair for the dramatic," she teased, "but I did want to share my good news with all of you together at one time." Olivia related her dream with picturesque descriptions, trying to convey the depth of her perceptions and feelings. She also injected humor—quite unlike her usual speeches she'd given at many charity events through the years. Her delight with the character of Jesus peppered her talk, to the extent that everyone in the room had a clear image of a smiling Savior lavishing unconditional love on a novice at receiving it.

"I have no clear word on whether there will be horses in heaven," she winked, "but heaven has become a very dear place to me. I long to see it again soon, and I know I will." The room grew hushed again. "But I couldn't leave you without thanking each of you for every word and deed that led me to my Master's side—on horseback, no less."

She enumerated a few such experiences, mentioning Jan Dyer's belief in the power of a person to change, Brianne's courage and faith in the face of cancer, Kathy's humble forgiveness of her husband's murderer, Parker's encouragement to seek forgiveness for herself and from others, and all the acts of kindness she'd received from a family of Christ-followers. "The theme of grace flows through you all," she concluded. "I now understand a bit of its meaning." She paused to collect herself.

"I've had several days—and several more conversations with Jesus—to consider my response. Tonight I am announcing that I, too, accept His gift of mercy. I am a Christ-follower." Shouts of jubilation echoed around the room.

"I want what time I have left to count. Alexis will be here this weekend.

I hope to love her into the kingdom, as you've done me. She's looking for meaning and relationship—she just doesn't know it yet. Give her time and patience." Olivia put her index finger to her lips, as though sharing a secret. Everyone grinned and nodded.

The last car pulled from the parking lot and cleanup began. Olivia—snug in her bed where her sons had placed her and where Louisa had seen to her comfort—smiled into the night's blackness with wonder and awe. All those years of dreading the dark, the endless nights of insomnia and restlessness. Now it gave her the solitude to talk with her Savior. She thought their conversations might go on forever.

Back at the Brooks house, Jan Dyer rehearsed the evening's events with all the participants as though she were a veteran reporter. "I imagine each of us there wondered who would have the honor of ushering Olivia into the kingdom. Would it be me? Would it be you?" She lifted a bony finger toward heaven. "Wouldn't you know, He'd do it Himself! I told you God was up to something."

21

Ty's three-day suspension had ended. With the excitement of his grandmother's surprise dinner party and announcement of her new relationship with Christ, there had been no time for *the talk* with his parents that Ty so dreaded. Surprisingly, he'd heard nothing from his mother or father or his sister. It seemed as though the family had agreed to a truce without his knowing the white flag had been raised.

After school he had to make up for missing track (although he'd spent most of his free time sprinting and working out), so he was late to dinner. His mom heated a plate for him and then left the kitchen, mumbling something about a financial report she needed to go over with his dad before tomorrow's Sloan Foundation board meeting.

While he was eating, Holly came through the back door with a drugstore sack in her hands and headed toward her room. "I'm packing." She hurled the announcement into the air as she zipped past him. She was flying back to D.C. on Saturday. He wondered how packing could take four days. Unless she had to do laundry. He thought about the cluttered floor of his bedroom. He might make some points with his mom by putting in a load of his own stuff. Finished with his meal, he stacked his dishes in the dishwasher and went to ask Holly if she'd need the washer.

"Come in," Holly announced to his knock. Ty opened the door to find her bed covered with clothes.

"Hey, I thought I was the messy one." He stepped over several pairs of shoes.

"I can't just put these in a suitcase," she fussed. "I've got to separate what I'll need for the next two days from what I'll need when I get there to what I'll just leave in my closet. And, of course, which shoes go with what, and the jewelry or scarves and jackets ..."

"Okay, I get it," he mumbled. "Do you need the washer?"

Startled, Holly asked, "No, do you? Since when did you volunteer to do laundry?"

"Since now, Miss Perfect." He started out the door when Holly stopped him.

"I'm sorry ... I didn't mean to sound insulting. Or, maybe I did. I apologize." Holly sat on her bed amidst the collection of clothing. "Can we talk?"

"I guess," Ty muttered. He dropped into the papasan chair. "What'da'ya wanna talk about?"

"Well, for one thing, I'm not perfect. I'm bossy, and impatient, and self-centered. I'm sneaky and too curious for my own good. Shall I go on?"

"Yeah. I'm kind of enjoying this."

"I love you more than words can convey. But I don't always show it. In fact, I've been very angry with you the past few days. But that's gone now. Just like Mom used to say when we were kids: 'Let me know when you've worn out your mad talk.' And she'd walk away."

"I think I've worn out mine, too." Ty shifted uncomfortably in the squishy chair.

"Can we be friends again?" They linked pinkies, just like in their younger days. "And as friends, I was wondering, could we talk about what happened?"

"You mean the drug sting?"

"Yeah. Was it Guillermo you met at the trail that night I saw you?" When Ty nodded, she asked, "Were you ... what were you exchanging?"

"Plans, ideas about how to pull this off. We didn't want stuff on our cell phones or emails."

"Oh. I wondered."

"Sorry I lied about it. I didn't want you involved ... in case."

"So! You did know the danger involved! Why did you agree to do this?"

"Agree? It was my idea. I talked Guillermo into it."

"But—"

"I know. You don't get it. Holly, everyone else in the family is fighting the drug trade except me. Even with your school load, you volunteer at the DC office. I was doing squat. It was important to me to make a contribution."

"But why did Uncle Parker's book upset you so much? It was supposed to be a tribute to those who'd been freed from addiction."

Ty sat in silence. Finally, he sighed. "Because of the dedication … to me, of all people. To the only one who wasn't doing squat, remember? I was embarrassed and ashamed."

"No one felt that way about you," Holly stammered.

"I felt that way. It mattered to me."

Holly went with her instincts and threw herself on her brother, knocking him backwards with her bear hug. When she finally untangled herself, she sat on top of him. "And now, for my second reaction to your brilliant plan, bro." That's when she reached for a pillow from her bed and smacked him in the head. He responded in kind, and the pillows started flying.

Startled by the sound of the washing machine filling with water, Brianne headed for the laundry room. Surely, the plumbing pipes had burst. Instead, she saw her son calmly putting in clothes from an overfilled basket.

Seeing her quizzical look, Ty shrugged, as though doing laundry was an everyday occurrence for him. He followed her back to her office. Curiosity made him ask, "I've been wondering … On the morning Uncle Parker came to talk to me, what did he say to you on his way out?"

She kept her eyes focused on her computer as she replied, "To leave you alone. To give you some time."

Ty took in the information. Uncle Parker had more sensitivity than he'd thought.

"So I did as he asked," his mom continued. "Was it helpful?"

"Yeah. Thanks."

Silence hung in the air as he tried to think of something to say—some way to help her understand his actions. "Mom, I'm sorry I scared you. I never thought I'd wind up in jail … or suspended from school."

Brianne turned her chair around. "I know. But thanks for saying it."

Ty stood awkwardly. "I was trying to help."

"So I hear." She rose and put her arms around his waist. He hugged her tightly.

"I love you."

"I love you too, son."

When Gavin got home, he could see the lights in Brianne's office and in the kids' bedrooms. He pulled his car into the garage, gathered his coat and briefcase, and headed for his wife's domain. She looked up as he entered and gave him a wide grin.

"You've had a long day. Want some warmed up dinner?"

"Why do you think I came home?" he teased. He kissed her and slung his coat and briefcase across the loveseat. He settled into an armchair, wishing it were his comfy recliner. "First, I have to find the energy to get to the kitchen."

Brianne rolled her chair to his side and placed his hand next to her cheek. "I wish you didn't have to work so hard. We've still got to look at these financial reports for tomorrow."

"Rats!" Gavin kissed each of her fingers.

"Ty apologized tonight for scaring me half to death."

"Oh, really?" He sighed and settled back in the chair. "I've been putting off talking to him. Parker's the one who gets why Ty felt he needed to prove something to us. But that night at the jail, I realized I don't know my own son as well as I thought I did. I didn't even know who his friends were. I need to spend some serious time getting acquainted with the almost grownup version of Tyler. Figure out what his interests are. Maybe he should talk to Parker again."

"Why don't we see if they can get together after the board meeting tomorrow? And if he wants to speak to Ty alone."

"Good idea. I'll shoot him a text. Now about that plate of food …"

"I'll bring it in here. Don't move a muscle."

"Good. I really, really don't think I can make it to the kitchen."

22

The board meeting had gone well. Parker found himself whistling as he climbed out of his truck and headed into the burger place where he'd arranged to meet Ty. He couldn't remember when he'd eaten his last hamburger. Kathy guarded his diet like a bloodhound on the trail of grease.

Ty was sitting in a corner booth, looking as though he'd lost his only friend. Poor kid! Parker hoped to make him feel as comfortable as possible. Ty's predicament had softened his heart toward his nephew, whom he'd really taken for granted. Maybe they all had.

"Hey." Parker slid into the booth across from him.

"Hey. I ordered for us. Hamburgers with all the trimmings. You get to choose your drink." Ty took a sip of his frosted mug of Root Beer.

"How'd you know I was planning to order a burger?"

"Holly's not the only family member with instincts. Besides, I was going to make you. If I have to be here talking to you, you have to eat like the regulars."

"Got it." Parker ordered iced tea. "How's track? Competition start soon?" By the time they'd discussed the various upcoming meets, burgers had arrived and the two dived in as though they'd been on a three-day fast. The chocolate ice cream sundaes were Parker's final break with reality. He patted his stomach. "We need to do this more often," he joked.

Ty laughed at the prospect. "Naw. You'd never give up being so buff. All the ladies staring at you …"

Parker threw back his head and laughed. At Ty's age, he'd wondered if he'd ever get a date, much less women's admiring looks. By the time he'd married, all his friends had teenagers.

He was about to shift to the subject of their meeting when Ty did it for him. "I read the chapter in the book you wrote about your story ... about your growing up years and your problems with your dad. I knew most of it—probably from hearing your testimony a thousand times."

Parker groaned, realizing the truth of Ty having sat through more than his share of his uncle's fundraisers.

"I guess I'd never put the pieces together—how you felt about not measuring up to your dad's expectations. All those years of his put-downs. Not accepting your becoming a doctor."

Parker nodded, not sure what to say. Ty kept going. "Then, to make matters worse, you began the Sloan Foundation with the money from Grandmother Sloan's will—money your father fought you for in court. That must have been tough."

"Yeah. In some ways, I felt I was betraying him."

"I guess I always thought you and Dad had it pretty easy—living in that great big house, driving fancy cars, going to medical school and law school. I guess I made it into a kind of perfect life. I didn't understand the pressure you faced. I sure didn't know what it must've been like to grow up without hugs and, you know, all the love and support my parents give me."

Ty paused. "When you talked about those 'study buddies,' the little pills that helped you get through medical training, it reminded me of why Guillermo and I were so angry at the drug trade. How people start using and then can't stop ... and how places like the Sloan House are often their only hope."

Gathering his courage for what was coming next, he continued, "I'm sorry I resented you ... actually, envied you ... made you into somebody you're not. In the book you talk a lot about personal responsibility, and how we all make choices—even when we've been dealt a sorry hand. I've made some bad choices. I haven't respected myself. Haven't tried to be the person God created me to be. I just wanted to be like other people, people who seemed to know where they were going and how to get there. I didn't like me very much ... or maybe at all."

A tear trickled down his cheek. He brushed it away with his sleeve and looked out at the parking lot. Parker felt clueless about whether or when to jump in and say something. He let several minutes tick by before answering.

"You've expressed your feelings very well, Ty. I could never have done that at your age. You are light years ahead of where I was—what I understood— at age seventeen." Ty seemed to brighten at the commendation.

"I need to apologize, too. First, I didn't ask your permission about the dedication. Maybe if I had, we could have had this talk months ago. Maybe you wouldn't have thought you had to prove yourself to any of us. Second, I've taken our relationship for granted. I want to spend more time with you—if you'll feed me burgers." They exchanged a grin.

"Finally, I want to assure you that God will open doors and lead you to his future for you—not mine or your parents' or Holly's—but to your unique role in his plan. Just let him know you're open to his direction.

"Hopefully, you won't have to find your way through the hard knocks I took. It doesn't seem all that long ago I was clueless as to what God's plan was for my life. And that plan may change tomorrow. But I know who's in charge."

Parker shifted his posture. "Ty, have you made that decision for sure? Do you know Who is in charge of you?"

Ty studied the remains of his sundae before replying. "I kinda lost my way there for a while, but now I'm back on the road. God's in charge."

"Good. Remember this: It's not what you do. It's whose you are."

Ty nodded.

"You're a fine person, Ty. I'm honored to be your uncle."

"And I'm proud to be your nephew. But can we get out of here before I embarrass myself again?"

"Sure, buddy. I presume you're picking up the check?"

"Yeah, right."

Parker caught the waitress's eye. In the parking lot, he thanked Ty for making their time together so much easier than he'd feared.

"I talked to Matt," Ty added.

"Matt? Kathy's son? Your cousin? In Phoenix?"

"Yeah. He pretty much told me what you'd say. And he also told me I was brainless if I messed up the good thing I've got going with you."

"Smart guy." Parker threw his arm around Ty's shoulder and walked him to his car.

"So no more jail stints or suspensions?" Gavin had his son cornered in the wing back chair in his home office.

"No, Dad."

"And you're going to invite Guillermo for dinner at our house? Soon?"

"Right."

"No more secrets?"

"Wait, Holly has lots of secrets."

"Just from you. I know her like a book."

"Sure. Sure you do."

"And always remember, I love you very much."

"Love you, too, Dad. … Oh, huh, I'd like a favor—if you have time."

"Son, I've got all the time in the world. What's up?"

"I want us to go see Pastor Frank. You know, our pastor when I was a little guy."

"Sure, Pastor Frank." Taken aback, Gavin rubbed his chin. "Gotta say I'm surprised."

"I've been thinking about it for a long time," Ty revealed. "God doesn't seem to want me to let go of it. The idea keeps bugging me. Maybe he's got something to say to me. 'A word from the Lord.'" Ty laughed uncomfortably. 'Religious talk' was not in his usual conversation— another thing he hoped to change.

"I'll make the arrangements. You know Pastor Frank is in assisted living."

Ty nodded. Maybe this was his worst idea ever. The two said goodnight and Ty headed back to his room.

Holly lay on her bed crosswise texting Hannah when her phone rang. She clearly recognized the tone she used for Blake's calls. Her heart beat faster. Unable to think of a reason to let it go to voicemail, she picked up. "Hi, Blake. What's going on?"

"Missing my sweetheart," he replied.

Holly tried to collect her thoughts. "I can't talk right now. I'm leaving in a few minutes."

"Oh. Are you and Hannah going somewhere?"

"No, actually I've got a date." She pictured a little devil sitting on her shoulder encouraging her to lie.

"An old boyfriend?" Blake sounded amused.

"No, a new one." As long as she was fibbing, she might as well make the story a good one.

"I'll bet I'm a better surfer." Now Blake was playing with her. She decided she was in as deep as she wanted to get.

"Sorry, Blake, I hear the doorbell ringing." She clicked off the phone.

Holly resumed her texting. Then she scrolled her social media. She picked up Uncle Parker's book and began reading. *Pretty good stuff*, she thought. She could definitely hear her uncle's voice in the conversational writing style. A few chapters in, she grew tired. Before she could consider her options, her cell rang Blake's tune. Absent-mindedly, she picked up the call.

"Hi, there. I hope I'm not calling too late."

Holly jerked her head off the bed shams. "Uh ... no, I guess not."

"Saw a great theater play tonight. Wish you'd been here to see it with me."

Holly stammered, "Sorry I missed it."

"How was your date—you know, the new guy?"

"Blake, don't be silly. I'm not going to talk about that." Inwardly, she groaned. *Why did I lie about that? I wasn't on a date. That's what I get for fibbing.*

Blake chuckled, "Oh, a mystery date. I love mysteries."

"Look, I was just getting into bed. Call another time ... er, I mean, don't call. I'll see you later ... or not." Totally frustrated with herself, she clicked off. She felt sure Blake was laughing at her. With that, she tucked herself in, pulling her comforter over her ears. Then she remembered she was still dressed.

23

Pastor Frank couldn't have been more pleased when he heard Gavin and Tyler were coming for a visit. Of course, he was free. In fact, he insisted they come. He tried to visualize Ty as a nearly grownup seventeen-year-old, but all he could remember was a shy youngster hanging on to his mother's leg while his boisterous older sister claimed the limelight.

And Gavin—my, the thrill of his coming to know the Lord. And the turnaround in his lifestyle. It would be great to see the middle-aged version of that hot-tempered young man caught in the web of alcoholism and drug use. Parker had stopped by to see him several times since his retirement, but he couldn't remember a visit from Gavin. But, then, his memory wasn't all that reliable these days.

He tidied up his small apartment and put some soft drinks in the refrigerator. His favorite Bible lay in its usual place on the coffee table. When his doorbell buzzed, he shuffled to the door and greeted his visitors warmly.

Now the guys sat with soft drinks in hand in his comfortable old armchairs while he sat on the couch. Naturally, they talked about Vanderbilt basketball and happenings within the church. It delighted him to hear that Gavin's mother was now a Christ-follower. They stopped to pray for Brianne as she battled this latest round of cancer.

"So, what brings you here?" the perceptive pastor asked.

Gavin looked over at Ty, who was trying to form the words to answer the question. Ty began with his sense that God wanted him to talk to Pastor Frank about his feelings of inadequacy. He explained about Parker's book and the dedication—how it had increased his sense of not being a part of "the family business"—The Sloan Foundation's efforts to combat drug use. How he'd tried to change that through breaking up a drug bust and, finally, his talk with Uncle Parker, who'd always seemed to him to be perfect.

At that point, Pastor Frank jumped in. "Oh, no, son. You don't ever want to settle for perfect."

Ty looked startled, but his eyes said 'tell me more.' The old gentleman continued.

"When Jesus said, 'Be perfect,' the word should be translated 'be whole, be complete.' The quest for the state of perfection leads to perfectionism. Perfectionism is a diseased state. It demands we get things right, do right, be right—a terrible taskmaster. We live in fear of being wrong. You don't ever want to be called 'perfect.'"

Pastor Frank sipped his Coke while the Hamilton men sat stunned. He continued, "What you want to be is *whole.* When you are complete in Christ, you are willing to fail, to change perspective with changing circumstances. In other words, to be led. Such a person doesn't ask, 'What does God want me to *do*?' but rather 'Who does God want me to *be*?'

"You see, perfectionism is based on performance. It leads to self-confidence based on your own ability to succeed. Wholeness is based on your identity in Christ. You act out of confidence in Him, not in yourself."

Ty soaked in his words. Pastor Frank was comfortable with silence, and he made his guests feel comfortable with it, also. After a while, Ty spoke up. "That makes sense to me. I wanted to be someone I'm not, and—well, truthfully—I was angry at God, who made me like I am. Now I've got to get comfortable in my own skin. I need to ask the 'who does God want me to be' question instead of the 'what to do' one."

Gavin nodded. "That's a good word for all of us. In the kingdom, doing follows being."

Ty stood and held out his hand. "Thank you, Pastor Frank. I knew God was sending me here." He shook hands with the man who'd helped generations of his family grow in Christlikeness.

After the two visitors left, Pastor Frank dropped to his knees—not an easy thing for him to do these days. He praised God that even in his old age he could be a part of the Hamiltons' journey of faith. What an honor.

❧

Brianne completed her simulation visit for SBRT on Friday, the day before Holly was to leave for school. She emerged from radiology looking like the champion she had always been. The Brooks, the Dyers, Parker, and Kathy waited with Gavin for her to give an indication of how the procedure had gone. Her wink and smile produced cheers all round. Dr. Givens was right behind her and greeted the family in the waiting room. "If this procedure does what we hope, she won't need further treatment." He turned to Brianne, "But follow-up, definitely. We'll see where we go from here."

"Hopefully, to the Caribbean," Gavin grinned. The group cheered the idea.

At the curb Gavin helped Brianne into their car, which Ty had waiting for them in the drive-through. "And now, M'Lady, we're all taking you to dinner. Unless you'd rather eat take-out."

"Let me think about that NO!" She leaned against the headrest and closed her eyes. "I'm picturing a juicy steak covered in mushrooms with garlic potatoes and a nice salad."

Gavin shouted directions to the other family members, who headed for their cars. As Tyler inched out of the circular driveway, Brianne pulled down the visor mirror and freshened her makeup. "I hope Holly hasn't had any trouble picking up Aunt Alexis at the airport."

From the driver's seat, Ty piped up, "If so, we'd have heard about it by now."

"Is she joining us at the restaurant?" Brianne asked.

"Yes," Gavin replied, "and Aunt Alexis, too, if she wants to come."

Brianne sighed, "It will be the last time all of us will be together until … well, we don't know when. Meme and Papa Dyer head home next week. And Holly won't be back until spring break."

"Peace and quiet on my end of the hall." Ty leaned against the back seat cushion and smiled. "No giggling. No cell phones ringing at all hours of the day and night. No shrieking, 'I've nothing to wear!'" He used a high pitch voice to imitate his sister, sending his parents into gales of laughter.

"Don't make your mom cry," Gavin teased. He laced his fingers through his wife's. Their glance said it all. Holly would be sorely missed.

&

Although the Hamiltons would rather have gone straight home from dinner, they couldn't refuse the invitation from Brianne's parents to drop by for dessert and one of Layton's surprises. Nana had baked her plum cake, the crowd favorite.

After eating, Layton escorted them to his man cave, which had been carved out of the original design for the extension of Amy's Interiors, Nana's home décor showroom and office. The sign on the door hadn't changed for almost 40 years: MAN CAVE: Keep Out. The warning had been marked with a colored red X and childish handwriting: Come on in.

"I've got a couple of additions to my trophy case I want to show you."

24

The Brooks/Hamilton clan moved toward the back wall of the man cave. A large trophy case took up the space between the two windows. "As you know, I keep the family's 'trophies of grace' on the top two shelves." He pointed to the trophies.

The bottom shelves contained various trophies and framed certificates each of the Brooks had won at fishing and sports tournaments, baking and art contests at the state fair, and Brianne's participation medals from every elementary grade.

Layton directed the group's attention to Amy and Brianne's trophies for *forgiveness* and *endurance*. After Brianne's recent diagnosis, he noted that Brianne was still in the process of *enduring the race set before her*. He picked up two other trophies and reviewed the stories behind Myra Norwell's trophy for *peace* after her battle with cancer and Abigail Sloan's trophy for *faith*. She'd believed in Parker rehabilitation while he was still in prison. As a result, she'd left him her estate. With the money, he had been able to establish The Sloan Foundation.

Layton turned to Meme Dyer, who stood erect but with quivering lip. He told the story of how Meme had continually refreshed the family's *hope* during the dark days of Brianne's cancer. Brianne placed an arm around her grandmother's shoulder. "Meme always said, 'God's up to something in this family.' And she continues to be right." Then Parker bowed his head at Layton's mention of his *freedom* award. "We are set free to serve," Layton concluded.

Ty had stood on one foot and then another as his grandpa talked.

Everyone had heard these tales of valor at least a million times, but Grandpa insisted that the retelling of the stories built their faith muscles. He couldn't have been more surprised to hear his name called.

"Come closer, son," Grandpa insisted.

Ty shuffled a few feet to where his grandpa stood. "I've just inscribed a trophy for you, and I want to present it now." Ty's eyes widened to twice their normal size. "It's for *courage*—courage to put yourself in danger for the good of others. To 'fight the good fight' as St. Paul said in a battle against drug trafficking, to which your family has given its life. But it was also a battle for courage within you—to find your true self and to live out the uniqueness of who you are. We're proud of you, son."

Ty, speechless and overwhelmed, took his grandpa's extended hand, which morphed into a hug. Everyone clapped, and his dad stepped forward to wrap him in another hug. "Th ... thanks," he finally muttered as he stepped away from the spotlight.

"I've got another new trophy I've added to my collection. Gavin, since you're standing right here"— he motioned him closer to his side — "would you please accept this trophy on behalf of your mother, Olivia Hamilton." Gavin tilted his head in surprise.

"Olivia deserves the award for *mercy*. She's claimed God's mercy in redeeming her sins and washing her as white as snow. She's asked her family for mercy—that supernatural power of forgiveness—and you've given it to her. And now she's asking God for His mercy to be extended to Alexis. And I'd like to add my prayer for mercy for my brother Kyle. May God grant these petitions."

Slowly, he put the trophies back where they belonged and shut the doors. Parker wept silently. Kathy handed him a tissue. Gavin and Brianne moved to join the two in an embrace. Then Layton led them in a prayer thanking God for the mercy each of them had received at His loving hands.

The family ambled to the living room, where they grabbed their jackets and purses. Words seemed inadequate, but hugs conveyed their feelings. The end to a wondrous day.

Back at home, Holly settled into her papasan chair for a final goodbye with her best friend. When Hannah picked up the call, Holly began in her usual way.

"You won't believe how Aunt Alexis looked. I'm still in shock that I got to pick her up at the airport."

"That's because the rest of the family was waiting at the radiology lab, remember? And hello, Holly."

"Hi, I know, but really. I felt so, so adult! And of course, I spent the whole morning trying to decide what to wear. I didn't want to look like I was trying to impress her."

"I know what you wore. We talked it through last night. You didn't change your mind, did you?"

"No, of course not."

"Then, get on with it. How did she look?"

"I wouldn't have even recognized her if she hadn't given me her location. For one thing, she's a redhead now. Can you believe it? She's had gorgeous blonde hair all her life."

"I suspect a few gray hairs were cropping up. A lot of women change their color about her age. What, early 50s?"

"I guess. She had on leggings and this short skirt—I swear her legs are longer than my whole body—and high heels with all these straps."

"Sounds just like me when I travel." Both of them giggled.

"Her jacket was cream colored, or winter white, not sure which, with a matching long coat slung over her shoulder and this Gucci® bag."

"Okay, okay, I think I've got the picture. Skip to the part about what she's like."

"Well, when she got in the car, you'll never guess what she asked me? Go ahead, guess."

"Holly, it's eleven o'clock, and you have to get up at dawn to catch your nine o'clock flight. Cut to the chase. I might even have a guy calling me later tonight. We've been texting all evening."

"Who?"

"My brother in Afghanistan. Get on with it."

"Oh. Well, she asked what had happened to her mother—why her mother was talking so funny. She wondered if we'd noticed how loony she'd become! Isn't that fantastic?"

"That your aunt thinks your grandmother is loony?"

"No—hey, stop teasing me! Alexis knows something's happened to Grandmother. I just played along, acting surprised. Grandmother made me promise I wouldn't tell Alexis about her decision to follow Christ. She wants to, well, warm her up to it, you know?"

"That's really exciting. I can't wait to hear how that goes. How long is she staying?"

"I don't think she's in any hurry to get back to Italy. Not sure Don Juan is still in the picture. You should have seen all the luggage she brought. It's a wonder the plane could fly. Must have cost her a fortune in baggage fees."

"How did you get it in your mom's car?"

"Oh, she had it delivered. What a relief!"

"So, did you see your grandmother?"

"No, Louisa met us at the door and told us she'd retired early. I think she wanted to have all day tomorrow to explain herself, if you know what I mean. I invited Aunt Alexis to join the rest of the family at the steakhouse for dinner, but she said she was tired from the trip. Honestly, those Hamilton women just don't *do* relationships! We'll bring her around soon enough!"

"So, maybe I'll meet her sometime. You're coming home for spring break, aren't you?"

"Oh, yeah. Especially if Mom … if the treatment … well, I'm only a couple of hours away."

"Sure. Everything's going to be fine."

"Of course." Holly hesitated. "Be sure and tell that handsome corporal of yours hello for me. And remind him to stay safe."

"Will do. And I'll be praying for Alexis."

"Thanks. Meme Dyer has the throne of God pretty well surrounded, but it won't hurt to add your two cents."

"What a compliment. Is Blake meeting you at the airport in D.C.?"

"Yeah. He's riding the subway to the airport, then we'll ride it back to my dorm. He wants to help with my luggage."

"Sure he does. It's all about the luggage," Hannah laughed. "Hey, just enjoy the relationship, OK? You don't have to decide right now if it's forever."

"Good advice. I guess I could relax a little. Give him some slack."

"Ya think?"

Holly sighed, "I can't believe the holidays are over. I'll miss you."

"I'm only a text away. Love you."

"Love ya too. Bye."

25

Ty awoke Saturday morning to the banging of closet and bathrooms doors. Holly's play-by-play of her final preparations and his mom's laughter echoed across the hallway. It would seem strangely quiet in his room without his sister's comings and goings.

Soon he'd have to get dressed and head for the school track. The practice run this morning was mandatory, preparation for the meet next weekend at Hillsboro High, the in-town rival. After his three-day suspension, he didn't want to be late.

Still, it felt good to lie in bed and put off the goodbye scene with Holly. He'd never admit he wished he could see his sister off at the airport. A lot had changed between them in the month she'd been home. Good stuff. A new appreciation of how much they cared about each other.

He smiled to himself as he thought about her funny re-enactment of meeting Alexis at the airport last night. Yes, it would seem very quiet around here for the next couple of months.

Ty threw off his sheet and planted his feet on the carpet. Donning a tee shirt, he headed across the hall to say goodbye to Holly. He gave her a hug and a slobbery brotherly kiss on the cheek. As she wiped it away, she whispered in his ear, "I'm glad you found your place in 'the family business.'"

"Getting there," he whispered back.

Olivia lay propped against the pillows on her bed. She'd asked Louisa to send Alexis in to see her as soon as her daughter was up and about. Today her breathing was labored, not encouraging when she felt she had so much to share.

She adjusted her covers and smoothed back her gray hair. Alexis would sleep late, she knew— jet lag and habit combined. Her thoughts drifted to yesterday's visit with Jan Dyer.

Jan had called to ask if she could stop by. Her daughter Amy was delivering samples to a real estate broker a few houses away, and she could drop her off. Olivia agreed, eager for a diversion from the boredom of illness. She'd asked Clarissa to set up a tea service in the sitting area of her bedroom while she changed into a flowing kimono.

Jan had arrived with fresh flowers, a stack of inspirational books, and note cards with a designer pen. At 90-plus years of age, she'd taken a moment to catch her breath after climbing the winding staircase to the second floor. "I'm so delighted Alexis is on her way home," Jan had begun. "What a wonderful opportunity the good Lord has provided you. You can share your good news about your new relationship with Christ as well as with your family."

Olivia had mentioned her nervousness about "getting it right," to which Jan had exclaimed, "Oh, pshaw! There's no such thing. My dear, just be yourself and share from your heart. Trust God to steer the conversation. You're a seed planter. Hopefully, you'll have time to do some watering, too. But the Lord brings the harvest. That's a promise."

Today Olivia was "resting in the promise" as she awaited Alexis' appearance. Yesterday, when Jan left, she'd said something that had made a lasting impression: "God's still up to something in this family."

She was counting on it.

Gavin looked at his feet for the umpteenth time, stalling for time with his daughter before she headed for the security line, already snaking around the last strand of rope at the busy airport. Brianne was repeating all the motherly advice she'd given so many times since Holly left for college.

"I'm glad Blake will be there to help you get to your dorm," she was saying. Gavin's mouth turned downward as he thought about the senior student who was so eager to see his freshman daughter. But he chose not to mention his reservations. Holly could probably recite them verbatim.

He interrupted his wife, "Holly, I hid chocolate all over the house last night. Too bad you won't be here to find it." He smiled smugly.

"Wanna bet?" Holly opened her shoulder purse to reveal a plastic bag filled with candy bars. All three burst out laughing. "Simple curiosity will take you amazing places. I left a few for you, but you'll have to find them."

"Got me," her dad admitted. "With that defeat in mind, let's pray." The trio linked hands as Gavin led them in prayer for Holly's travel, relationships, and academics in the new semester. Mostly, he thanked God for the blessings of the holidays, for family, and for his mother's salvation. He closed by asking God to prepare the way for Alexis to hear her testimony and receive Christ as her Savior, also.

"Hugs and kisses." Holly enveloped her parents in a bear hug.

"You're still my favorite Christmas present," her dad waved as she turned toward the security line. She looked back and blew him kisses.

"When you get to DC, say hello to the President." Brianne pulled Gavin away. Soon, they were in his car heading for home, their hands intertwined over the console between them.

Brianne tossed her strawberry curls and nestled into the seat cushion. "Can you believe?" she began. "Only four weeks ago I had cancer and didn't know it. Tyler was emotionally a thousand miles away from us. And you had almost no relationship with your mother. And now—in a matter of weeks—our lives have changed forever."

"Pretty amazing, huh?"

"Once again, I wondered why I had to have cancer. Isn't the third time supposed to be a charm?"

Gavin furrowed his brow. "Meaning?"

"If I hadn't felt ill, Holly wouldn't have gone to see your mother in the hospital and, as a result, begun a brand-new relationship with her. Olivia wouldn't have asked me questions about my health that led to our first conversation about my faith. We wouldn't have shared the mutual need for God's healing in our lives. My vulnerability gave her a chance to be vulnerable.

"Alexis might not have come home if I'd been able to care for your mother. Now she'll hear her mother's plea for forgiveness and her new faith journey. I know God used all of us in your mom's journey to salvation. But I'm glad I could contribute a small part. Still taking the test of endurance."

Gavin smiled at the reference to her dad's trophy case. He kissed her hand.

Blake Chandler rolled two large suitcases out of the subway station while Holly struggled to upright a carry-on bag. Readjusting her shoulder bag over her heavy jacket, she shouted, "Hey, wait for me."

Blake motioned to her luggage, "How did you ever think you'd get all this to your dorm without me?"

"Oh, there's this new invention called taxis," she shouted above the traffic. Slowly, they made their way from the Georgetown subway exit toward the campus. Once there, Holly begged to stop at a bench near the flight of stairs to her dorm's main entrance.

"Just because you're a muscled California beach boy doesn't mean the rest of us can keep up." She gazed at his bronzed face, wavy blonde hair, and green eyes. "Do you stay tanned year 'round?"

"Pretty much. Looks like you haven't seen the sun in ages. Did you stay indoors for a month?"

"Pretty much," she copied. She drew in a breath. "Isn't the cold air delicious?"

"Forgot to taste it," he teased. "So, your Nashville reports were kind of sketchy. Instead of the jumbled, emotional, exaggerated tales of yore, I'd like to hear the saga start to finish." He poked her in the ribs.

She poked back. "You lawyers are all the same. Logical, step-by-boring step. Just the facts, ma'am." She let her jab sink in. "Do you want it all now, or after you've fed me?" She batted her eyelashes as though he'd be hard to talk into a lunch date.

Later, after spaghetti at their favorite café, they sipped coffee as she recounted the story of Meme and Papa's surprise visit, Ty's great adventure, their growing closeness, and her mom's and Grandmother Hamilton's health crises. Best of all, she shared her grandmother's salvation.

Blake took it all in as though he were gathering evidence for a trial.

When she finished, he admitted, "Of course, I'd heard bits and pieces—when I could finally get you to pick up my calls." His pouty-face was pretty convincing. "That's a lot to go through in a short amount of time."

She nodded, lost in the memories.

"So, what's your summation to the jury?" His green eyes sparkled once again.

Holly's brown ones grew misty. "God is real. He's always at work in our lives. Mostly, we don't know what He's doing at any given point, and then—all of a sudden—we piece some of it together and stand amazed at His goodness. Best of all, He shows us grace when we least deserve it."

The green eyes became clouded. Blake took a sip of coffee. "The jury is requesting more evidence."

Holly knew Blake's faith was "squishy," having not grown up in a religious household. But she'd sparked his curiosity and some deep longing he'd yet to acknowledge.

"Oh, I've got plenty of evidence. God's always up to something in my family." She reached for his hand across the table, praying that someday God would show Himself to Blake—with all the evidence he'd need to witness a glimpse of His mercy.

26

With the Christmas holidays behind them, Meme and Papa were ready to get back to Florida. The two were running out of ideas for what to see and do in Nashville. With Holly back in DC and Ty finishing his last semester of high school, the excitement level at the Brooks/Hamilton homes had decreased significantly.

Amy and Meme were having herbal tea in the kitchen with nothing on the agenda. Amy leaned her elbows on the table. "I have an idea. How about I take you to see Olivia Hamilton? She's asked to see you before you head home."

Meme clasped her hands with pleasure. "I'd love that. I'll call Louisa and see if this is a good day for her." With that, Meme took her coffee and phone and ambled toward her favorite chair in the living room.

When Amy heard the phone click off, she asked, "Did you find out if Olivia is available for a visit this afternoon?" Meme told her the visit was scheduled for three o'clock. "I'll be glad to take you and pick you up. I need to say hello to my daughter's mother-in-law."

Layton and Phil breathed a sigh of relief. After entertaining family for more than a week, they were both ready for an afternoon nap.

When Amy pulled up to Olivia Hamilton's stately Belle Meade mansion, both Louisa and Clarissa were at the door to help Jan Dyer up the front steps and into the parlor on the first floor. Olivia sat in a wing-back chair dressed in flowery Oriental pajamas with matching slippers. "Please come in and have a seat," she said, motioning to a loveseat across from her.

Amy soon excused herself so the two older ladies could enjoy each other's company. Louisa fluffed the pillows behind Olivia's chair while Clarissa went for the tea set. When the ladies were settled with their cups and a selection of sweets, the faithful duo left the two alone. Jan Dyer was full of Christmas news. Olivia listened without much commentary. An uncomfortable silence settled between them.

"Tell me," Jan asked her friend, "What's on your heart today?"

Olivia looked at her feet, a slow blush creeping across her pale cheeks. "Alexis came home from Italy, and I was nervous as a cat. I wanted so much to share with my daughter my newfound faith in Christ and to ask her forgiveness for not having loved her as I should have." She stopped, a single tear escaping her right eye. Jan waited for her friend to continue.

"When I asked for her forgiveness for my poor mothering skills, she dismissed my concerns as though she'd never noticed. I'm afraid I've reared a duplicate of myself. She'll stay for my birthday in three weeks. Please tell me you'll be praying for her to forgive me."

"What did she say about your coming to believe in Jesus Christ?"

"I tried. I guess I'm fortunate she didn't have me committed to an institution. Who else would say she met Jesus riding on a Palomino horse?"

Jan laughed. She remembered Olivia's account of her dream vividly. In it, Olivia sat on the grass with her parents in a pastureland much like the horse farm where she grew up. A rider on a Palomino approached and introduced Himself as Jesus. "I've loved you with an everlasting love," Jesus said. Olivia felt the warmth in His eyes and experienced a glimpse of the mercy He was offering her.

Long unable to forgive her father for his unfaithfulness to her mother, Olivia had shielded herself from the affection of her family. Finally free to forgive and be forgiven, she had yielded all the hurt and pain to the only source of lasting comfort. Jesus became her Savior and Lord.

Olivia spoke up. "My husband Hollister died of a massive heart attack years ago without a personal relationship with Jesus. Now I am determined that my daughter Alexis will have the opportunity to make a life-changing decision to follow Christ."

Jan looked into Olivia's bright eyes. "Do you remember our last conversation?"

"Yes. You said I'm a seed planter, and the Lord brings the harvest. I'm still resting in the promise that He will do a mighty work in Alexis' life.

"He will," Jan replied. "But I also trust God for His timing. You can be sure He's still up to something in this family."

Holly's spring routine at Georgetown mirrored her first semester. Many of her courses were in fact continuations of the first. Her sights were set on spring break. Some of her campus friends were determined to lure her to a beach vacation. However, after the turmoil of her Christmas vacation, she just wanted a quiet week at home.

She wanted to see for herself her mother's progress in fighting this third battle with cancer. She looked forward to seeing Hannah. Her detective instincts led her to believe Hannah was dating someone. *Why can't she just admit it?* Holly wondered. In high school Hannah had dates to proms and special events but never a steady boyfriend. She always had her head in a book. Holly guessed opposites really did attract. She spent her free time in student clubs and all things social. She barely made it into the National Honor Society. Hannah, of course, was the president.

Spending time with Hannah gave her structure and stability she couldn't seem to manage on her own. In turn, Hannah claimed Holly added spice to her life. As her Nana would say, the one "fly in the ointment" for spring break was Blake. He wanted to come home with her. "My one chance to see the country music capital of the world," he whined. As March grew closer, his whining grew worse.

Finally, she called her father at his office to get his approval. She would have called her mother, but she would have said to talk to her father. Might as well get it over with.

"Absolutely not." Holly's dad used his courtroom voice. Generally, at that point the conversation ended. Holly knew she'd need more than a *no* to satisfy Blake.

With little hope of success (although she wasn't sure she wanted to entertain Blake on her laid-back spring break), she pressed on. "Why, Dad?"

"Because you're still a freshman in college. You don't need to be bringing boys home to meet your parents at this stage. It would send Blake the wrong message."

Holly couldn't really argue with that. Blake didn't need any encouraging signs. Like fly paper, he seemed stuck to her indefinitely. Not that she didn't enjoy his company. She just needed some space.

"Okay, I'll tell him we have other plans." She thought quickly. "Why can't the family go to Pigeon Forge?"

"Because your spring break doesn't match Ty's spring break."

Defeated, Holly agreed that Blake was a *no*, and moved on to other topics. When she clicked off the phone, all she had to do now was tell Blake. Suddenly, she needed chocolate.

When Holly rode the escalator down to baggage claim at the Nashville airport, she saw her brother standing there to meet her. Surprisingly, her parents were nowhere to be seen. She waved to him. As she approached the end of the escalator, she wondered if Ty would appreciate a hug. Maybe he was too manly for that now. Fortunately, he made the first move.

"Hi, sis." He grabbed her around the shoulders. With a purse and a carry-on bag in either hand, Holly was stuck. "Good to see you," she squeaked out. "Now let me go." Ty released her with a look of triumph and took her carry-on.

"I couldn't figure out which carousel your luggage would arrive on. Mom didn't give me much information about your flight."

"Oh, really? Did you volunteer for this assignment or were you forced to pick me up?"

"A little of both."

"So, are you saying the excitement of seeing me again wasn't your sole motivation?"

"Yes, of course." Holly playfully jabbed his shoulder. Ty explained, "Dad's in court and Mom had a doctor's appointment moved up unexpectedly. I had to talk my way out of track practice to be here."

They approached the carousel. Holly found a space near where the luggage would roll out. Her thoughts remained stuck on the idea of her mom being at a doctor's office. "Is Mom OK? Why the change in appointment?"

Ty shot her a mischievous grin. "How tempting to string you along with made-up medical jargon. Actually, her lung specialist changed the date. He will be in Hawaii next week with his daughter on spring break. I'll also be on spring break next week, but my parents haven't told me where we're going. I'm guessing the Caribbean."

Just then Holly watched her big suitcase come into view. They both lunged for it and together pulled it off the line. Ty rolled it away toward the exit with Holly hurrying behind him with her shoulder bag and carry-on. They headed to Ty's car and drove to the toll booth. Holly offered to pay, and her brother cheerfully accepted.

"No charge," the attendant announced. "You were within the thirty-minute window."

Holly grinned. "With the change you no longer need, we can pick up a smoothie."

"Save your money. I'll make you one at home."

Holly leaned her dark locks on the head rest. "I'm pretty sure you're not going to the Caribbean next week. Mom would have told me. Besides, when have you ever seen Dad take a vacation?" By this time, they were approaching I-24. Holly nodded toward the interstate. "More likely you're going to Murfreesboro." She laughed at her joke.

"Why did you mention Murfreesboro?" Ty asked.

Holly tilted her head toward him. "No reason."

"Did Mom or Dad mention anything to you about Murfreesboro?"

"No, Ty. It's just the closest town I could think of east on I-24. Am I supposed to know something special about the town? There are some cute shops on the courthouse square."

"I'll tell you when we get home." They rode in silence the few minutes it took to get to their home. Holly fumed at the idea she would be the last to know whatever secret awaited her.

Once home, Ty delivered a strawberry smoothie to her room where Holly was unpacking enough clothes for two weeks instead of one. Soon, she heard guitar strokes coming from Ty's room across the hall. The sound didn't seem to come from any electronic device. Her sleuthing led her to knock on Ty's door.

"Come in," he hollered. Holly tried, stepping over the clothing on the floor, until she cleared a space near her brother and plopped on the floor. Ty was strumming the guitar she remembered as a previous year's Christmas present. However, she'd never heard him play it or even pluck a few strings. Ty appeared to love the look of surprise on her face.

"When did you take up the guitar?"

"A couple of months ago. Uncle Parker thought it would be a good idea for me to have a hobby. Something besides track. I'm actually taking lessons." He played a few chords to get her reaction.

Holly took his strumming hand and examined it. Sure enough, the beginnings of callouses were forming on the ends of his fingers. "I'm impressed," she exclaimed. "So does this have anything to do with Murfreesboro?"

"Not really. You'll have to wait until Mom and Dad get home for that."

Her best wheedling got her nowhere. She sulked back to her room. At least talking to Hannah would change her mood.

"Hi, Hannah. What's his name?"

"Why, Holly. How nice to hear from you. Did you have a good flight home?"

"You're changing the subject. You know I've been dying to hear all about him."

Holly could hear Hannah's big sigh over the phone. Maybe she'd been too abrupt. *Ease into it,* she told herself. "How are your parents and Denny?"

Hannah laughed. "Girlfriend, you'll never win a subtlety contest. My family is fine, and his name is Seth."

"Seth what?"

"That's all you need to know at this point. Otherwise, you'll be checking him out on every social media site, class yearbooks, and the Department of Public Safety."

Holly pouted briefly. She had other covert methods. "So how did you meet?"

"It was all very romantic. At the public library. We were in the L through M aisle."

"That's something to go on. Who do I know with access to library card data?"

Hannah groaned. "Stop it, Holly. That's all you're getting from me."

"I don't know." Holly scratched her chin. "Seth is an unusual name. How many guys named Seth go to Peabody?"

"Did I say he goes to Peabody?"

"Oh, I get it. He's fourteen and a friend of Denny's. You have to pick him up until he can get a driver's license."

Hannah giggled. "Right on, Holly. You go with that." The young women planned to meet the following day to catch up with each other. "Just not about Seth," Hannah insisted. When they hung up, Holly reviewed the ways she'd learned to get information out of her best friend.

The phone rang almost as soon as she put it down. Of course, it was Blake. "Good news," he practically shouted into her ear. "Hope your trip went well. I'm at the Reagan airport as we speak."

Holly tried to absorb the news. Wasn't Blake stuck in DC for spring break? His parents lived in California and always said it was too far and too expensive to fly home for just a few days. Finally collecting her thoughts, she responded. "Wow! You're flying home?"

"Better than that. I have an interview with a New York law firm to be a summer intern."

"Good for you." Holly felt a sigh of relief coming on, but she squelched it. "Do I know the firm?"

"No, but your dad probably does. Let's wait until I get the job."

"You sound pretty confident. When would you start?"

"A week after graduation. You know my parents are coming for it. Maybe I'll get to show them around New York City as well as Washington DC."

Holly had just begun her inquisition of Blake when she saw her mom's car pass her bedroom window on the way to the garage. "Sorry. I've got to go. My mom just got home, and I haven't seen her yet. We'll talk later, OK?"

She signed off and headed down the hallway to intercept her mother.

28

The conversation around the Hamilton dinner table was lively, each interrupting the other to tell a story or relate information. From Holly's endless questions she learned her mother's checkup had gone well, Ty was rocking all his classes, and Guillermo had been to their home several times. In fact, her dad was so impressed with his Spanish that he was learning a few words and phrases. Her mom affirmed that The Sloan Foundation was doing so well that she was back to fulltime as the administrative assistant.

Ty brought up the touchy subject of Blake. "How did he take the news that he had been disinvited to Nashville?" he asked. Her father leaned in for her answer.

"Not happy about it, but he's not a quitter. He'll probably ask to spend the summer with us." Her parents shared some nervous laughter. "Actually, I'm joking. Believe it or not, he's flying to New York City for an interview with a law firm for a summer internship." Holly caught her parents exchanging looks.

"Isn't he off to Columbia Law School in the fall?" Ty asked. Holly nodded as she chewed a forkful of pork chop. "That's good, huh?" he continued. He looked toward his dad. "Blake gets a head start on other law students looking for jobs when school starts."

"Definitely. He's making a sharp move. Wonder how he got the interview?"

Holly silently guessed that Uncle Parker had something to do with it, although she had no way of knowing. She wondered if her dad had put his brother up to it. Just to keep them apart. With all eyes on her, Holly explained, "Our conversation got interrupted when Mom came home. That's all I know."

"Yes, and I enjoyed a few minutes with my daughter before I started dinner. Holly, don't you have plans for the summer too?"

"As for me, I'm thinking about staying in Washington when the semester ends. Uncle Parker needs my help since several of his interns are graduating, including Blake. Plus, I want to get a couple of classes out of the way. Then, I'll have a lighter load in the fall, and I can work more."

"Yeah, and we need you to make all the money you can," added Ty. "Don't forget that I'll be in college next fall too."

Holly's lips parted. That fact had actually slipped her mind. "Wow, Dad. Looks like you'll also need to work more."

He picked up his glass of tea and took a sip. "Fortunately, Ty actually applied himself to his studies"— he glared at Holly —"and has gotten a fat scholarship."

Ty folded his arms over his chest. He gave Holly a smug grin. "And you have no idea where I'm going."

Holly pursed her lips and stared at the ceiling for a few moments. "Does this have anything to do with Murfreesboro?" she asked.

Her dad exclaimed, "Why would you think that?" He turned to Ty, who shrugged his shoulders.

Holly sighed with pleasure that she'd figured out their surprise. She repeated a saying quite familiar to her family. "Simple curiosity will take you amazing places."

Her mom chimed in, "Go ahead and tell her, Ty, before she tells us."

Ty stuck out his chest. "I have a full track scholarship to Middle Tennessee State University—you guessed it—in Murfreesboro, Tennessee."

"Congratulations, little brother." Holly flew around the table and threw her arms around him. "Let's have a celebration."

Her dad agreed. "Don't I see an apple pie on the cabinet?"

The kids rose to clear the table while Mom cut the pie and Dad refilled their glasses.

Gavin lay in bed waiting for Brianne to join him. She shouted from the master bath, "Just taking off my wig and my fake eyelashes."

"Funny girl." He turned toward her voice with his head on his elbow. "I'd never have married you without your gorgeous red hair. Not sure about the eyelashes. I'll have to look more closely." After several more minutes had passed, he groused, "I think you're avoiding a conversation we need to have."

Brianne appeared in the doorway to their room with her face covered in a brown clay mask. With lips that barely opened, she eked out, "Why would you say that?"

Gavin chuckled. "Because you don't like to tell our children *no*. You've got a heart so big a bus could drive through it. But that's all right. I'll be the bad guy."

Brianne hurried to her sink and began scrubbing her face. With a towel in hand, she reappeared in the doorway. "What are you saying *no* to?" She sat down on his side of the bed.

"Holly has no business spending the summer in DC. She can always take classes at one of the fine universities in Nashville or online. I'm also sure Parker could find work for her here since Nashville is the headquarters of The Sloan Foundation. Plus, she doesn't need to be that close to New York City and Blake. They need a summer apart. For several more weeks, she's still a freshman."

Brianne folded the towel in her lap. "I see your point. Plus, Hannah is here, and our church. She'd be a great help with the college class. And living at home, we'd save the dorm fee, food, and travel expense. Let's move her home."

Gavin was about to congratulate himself on a win until Brianne added, "But let's not tell her now. She may change her mind, or we can always drop hints along the way."

"Why would we do that?"

"Because nineteen-year-olds don't respond well to parental edicts. And you happen to know her boss, who I'm sure could be persuaded that she needs to work from here."

"Brilliant." Gavin pulled her to him and gave her a sweet kiss. "Maybe when we met, I was also attracted to whatever is under your gorgeous hair." Brianne threw the towel toward the bathroom doorway, took off her prosthesis, and slipped in to bed beside him. They folded into each other's arms.

❦

Ty set off on his usual late-night run through the wooded area behind their house. He loved the stillness of the night, even with the chirping of the crickets and locusts. This time Guillermo wouldn't greet him at the stone bench. Now his friend came through the front door of their home, a welcomed guest. He'd pull his older model Chevy into their driveway where it would sputter to a stop.

Still, when Ty got to the bench he sat down. A flurry of thoughts ran through his mind as he reflected on the past three months since his brief stay in the holding cell at the precinct. The best part had been his new relationship with Uncle Parker. He'd thought that if his uncle ever knew how insecure and out of place he felt in the tight-knit family circle, he'd think less of him. Maybe have his book reprinted without the dedication to Ty.

Instead, the two met at least once a month for hamburgers and talked about stuff like what it really means to be a godly man; how to plan for the future; and ways to build his self-esteem. Uncle Parker wasn't preachy. He freely shared his own story of growing up without a healthy self-image, stories that hadn't made it into his book.

Another plus resulted from his and Guillermo's foolish decision to record an illegal drug purchase. He and his dad had a much better relationship. Dad had taken time off work—amazing in and of itself—to take him fishing. Now that Nashville's minor league season was starting, they planned to see at least three games. His mom wanted to go to one of them to get a greasy corndog! Life was good.

Topping it off was his full scholarship to MTSU. He loved track and field. The medals meant very little to him. The wind at his back, passing the competitors, feeling the runner's high—it was worth the hours of training.

Uncle Parker kept asking what God had to do with all of this. He didn't know. Similar to Eric Liddell's answer in the 1981 award-winning movie, "Chariots of Fire," Ty could only say, "God made me fast. And when I run, I feel His pleasure."

29

Holly and Hannah met at their favorite hangout just off the Vanderbilt campus. They sat outside on the wrought iron patio furniture despite the March wind. Hannah kept brushing back her brown hair as it blew across her face. Holly had pulled back her dark locks into a practical ponytail. As they ate, they carefully avoided talk of boyfriends, focusing instead on mutual friends and family members.

Hannah dropped her napkin into the plastic basket that had held her food. "What do you think of university life?" she asked Holly.

"Georgetown is so big it's been hard to make friends. However, I found a church near campus that serves students breakfast on Sundays before worship. Now that I'm plugged in to the group, I have several possible friends. But you are always going to be my BFF."

"Aww!" Hannah pretended to wave the compliment away. Holly returned the question, "How about you?"

"The college group at church is different. New students have replaced those who left us"— she gave Holly a disdainful glance —"including you. Several come from other countries. I'd like to get to know all of them better.

"I tutor students when I'm on campus and have free time between classes. At least, tutoring pays for incidentals, and I like teaching. After all, I'm an education major." She turned teasing eyes to Holly. "And your major?"

Hannah knew Holly didn't have a major. Furthermore, Holly didn't have a clue about her future life's work. She'd gone to Georgetown because

Uncle Parker offered her a part-time job at Sloan's DC lobbying firm. She'd wanted to explore a new city with a diverse student body.

Changing the subject, Holly surmised, "I guess with your homework and classes, not to mention the tutoring, you don't have much time for Seth."

"I wondered when we'd get around to Seth." Hannah planted her elbows on the table, daring her friend to probe for answers.

Holly was unfazed. "What with having to pick him up and have him home by nine o'clock, you hardly have time to see a movie."

"He's not fourteen!" Hannah shouted. She picked up the used napkin from the basket and threw it toward Holly. The wind carried it away.

Having satisfied herself that Seth was a real college student with a real career path and good morals, Holly drove home in her mom's car in a light rain. With the windshield wipers swishing back and forth, she replayed the conversation searching for any clue she might have missed to track Seth's identity.

Her ring tone interrupted her thoughts. The display assured her Blake was calling. She let the call go to voicemail, partly because of the rain, and partly because her father had threatened that if he ever caught her on her phone while she was driving … . He hadn't finished the sentence, leaving Holly's active imagination to go into overdrive. Besides, her car was in DC, and this car belonged to her mother. She instinctively slowed down.

Back at home she shared her lunch conversation with her mom and then headed to her room to call Blake. He answered immediately with an excited voice. "I got the internship."

Holly pictured Blake at his apartment window shouting for all of DC to hear. "That's great. And quick. You've only been in the city a full day!" With her thickest Southern dialect, she piled on the compliments. "Those law-wa-yers must a' reckonized yer outstandin' qualities, youngun. Yew'll go fer in this here life."

Blake laughed and attempted to acknowledge her praise in a similar fashion, "Thankie, missy. But there's a catch." He turned solemn. "My stipend will barely cover my expenses. I won't have anything left to fly to

DC to see my favorite Southern gal. Fortunately, the plane goes both ways. You can come see me."

Holly was stumped for a reply. Her parents would never let her fly to New York to see a guy they didn't want her to encourage. Finally, she mumbled, "We'll see. What happens now?"

"They'll set me up with a fellow intern who's also looking for lodging. Maybe together we can afford a nine by twelve studio apartment next to a construction zone." Holly giggled at the image of two guys bumping into each other in such a small space. "Meanwhile, I've got to come up with a deposit and a first month's rent."

"But you don't graduate until May?"

"My new boss says that's the only way the landlord will hold it for us. Do you think Parker would float me a loan on my good reputation with his firm?"

Silently, Holly thought, *He'd pay your entire summer's rent to get the two of us apart.* She wanted to be mad at her parents. But some still, small voice in her spirit told her there was probably some merit to their concerns.

"All you can do is ask," she advised. "I'll pray about it."

"You do that," he smirked. "What could it hurt?"

The remainder of Holly's spring break came and went with the speed of lightning. One highlight was her call to Meme in Florida. At Nana and Grandpa's house toward the end of the week, Nana had suggested the call. "Meme knows you're busy. If you could take a minute to talk to her, she'd love it."

Holly bowed her head in embarrassment that it had been weeks since the two of them had spoken. She lifted her eyes to Nana, a single tear edging its way down her cheek. "I feel terrible. I think of her almost every day."

Nana placed a comforting arm around her shoulder. "She understands. Don't feel bad. It would perk her up, though."

Holly picked up on the implication of Nana's words. "Does she need 'perking up'?"

Nana sighed. "Papa isn't doing so well. She's concerned about him, that's all."

Holly pictured her great-grandfather, a man of few words but a steady source of support to the entire family. When Papa spoke, he shared words of wisdom. He, too, was a prayer warrior but wasn't vocal about it like Meme. She shuttered to think about what his absence would mean to the family.

Nana shook her shoulder. "So, call her."

"I will later," she promised, afraid her emotions would upset Meme. "As soon as I get home. But I'm pretty sure I smell a plum cake in your oven and a timer just about to go off."

"The cake will need a few minutes to cool."

"Good. That's a few more minutes you and I will have to talk."

30

Once back home, Holly found several excuses to put off her call to Meme. Was it her sense of shame that she'd not called her for weeks? Or was it fear that she'd find out more about Papa's health than she wanted to know.

The first excuse was Ty. She heard him playing an unfamiliar song on his guitar. She had to step into his room to check it out. "I don't recognize the tune," Holly volunteered.

"I made it up." Ty looked down at his instrument, expecting Holly to say something snarky about his amateur songwriting. Instead, she complimented it and encouraged him to keep at it. As she left the room, she looked back at him and gave him a wink. Her brother had talent.

Then, her dad came home early. Holly followed him to his office. She found out he had a civic club meeting that night and had asked his wife for an early dinner. "Oh, no," Holly blurted out. "I just had two pieces of Nana's plum cake." Her dad assured her he was hungry enough to eat her dinner as well as his.

"Dad, Blake got the paid internship." He stopped in the middle of untying his necktie. Holly settled in an armchair. "He'll need a loan to pay for a down payment and first month's rent on an apartment—just until he gets his first paycheck. Then he can start paying back the loan. Do you think Uncle Parker could help him out?"

Her dad finished pulling off his tie and unbuttoning the top button of his shirt. "Parker keeps a two-bedroom apartment in NYC for Sloan Foundation employees and lawyers to meet with prospective donors and to visit the halfway houses we have in the state. I've stayed in it several times. Maybe Parker would offer him a bedroom until he can get a paycheck."

And check on his comings and goings, Holly thought. "So, will you alert Uncle Parker to the fact that Blake may call him? Plant the idea, hint, hint?"

"Actually, I'll see him at the meeting tonight. I'll think about it."

After dinner, Holly helped her mother clean the kitchen. When she told her she planned to call Meme, her mother spoke up. "Well, you'd better get after it. Remember, they are on Eastern Standard Time."

"Oops, I forgot." Holly put down the dishtowel and practically ran to her room. Her favorite site for calling anyone was her papasan chair. Once curled into position, she punched her favorites screen and soon had Meme on the line. Holly noticed at once how tired her great-grandmother sounded.

"Meme, I'm so sorry I called so late. I'll bet you're headed for bed."

"Darling, I'd stay up all night to talk to you. I hope all is well."

"Yes, I'm home for spring break. Actually, I leave on Saturday to go back to DC." The two soul-mates talked for several minutes about the Hamilton and Brooks family happenings before Holly broached the main reason for her call.

"How's Papa?" she asked, eyes shut tight preparing for Meme's answer.

"Today was a good day," she replied. "We were able to do a little gardening. He loved being outside before the summer heat settles in."

"Is—is Papa OK?"

"Well, dear, at our age the body doesn't always cooperate with our wishes. His arthritis slows him down a good bit. He gets winded easily and needs more rest than when we were trapsing through the mountains of Ecuador. Old age is a blessing, but it comes at a price."

Inwardly, Holly breathed a sigh of relief. Meme's description didn't seem too bad. When they finally said their goodbyes, Holly uncurled herself from the papasan and headed for her mother's study. She often worked into the night on Sloan business, especially when her husband wasn't home. "Mom?" Holly whispered at the doorway, not wanting to interrupt her on some tedious calculation.

"Come on in." Her mom clicked her mouse to save her document and turned her office chair to face the doorway.

Holly entered and sat on the loveseat. "Meme doesn't seem very concerned about Papa's health." Her mom raised her eyebrows as if to say tell me more. "Well, this afternoon at Nana's, she said Meme needed 'perking up.' I thought maybe Papa's health was failing."

"Rheumatoid arthritis is a serious condition. Papa needs a lot of care in just accomplishing daily tasks. I think Nana means Meme is tired. Helping him up and down is a strain on her system as well."

"But can't we do something? Get her a home health aide or someone to cook and clean?"

"Yes. She's asked for those services, but she's on a waiting list. Providers are hard to come by in South Florida, where many people need similar help. And there's not much government funding."

"Then, someone should go help her."

"Someone is," her mom explained. "Nana is leaving to spend six weeks with her as soon as Ty's spring break is over. She didn't tell you?"

"No." Holly thought back over their conversation. "She did mention something about Ty's spring break." Holly's eyes shot open. "Is the family going to the Caribbean?" Her mother's shocked expression confirmed that she knew nothing about such a trip. Once again, she'd jumped to a conclusion off of a chance comment from Ty.

Her mom explained that Ty, who had the only green thumb in the family, had agreed to help Nana with her spring plantings and other yard work. Holly groaned inwardly at her question and the simple truth of the matter.

"What happens after the six weeks is over? I'll finish my freshman year by then. Why didn't you tell me this when I first got home?"

"You had plans of your own, remember? Meme and Papa aren't your responsibility."

"Of course they are! They're family. When Nana gets back, I'll be free to go help. I'm strong, and I can cook a little, and clean, and wash clothes." Holly thought about the state of her room and the pile of dirty clothes that would need to be washed and packed by Saturday. "Well, I can *learn*," she voiced emphatically.

"I'll talk to Dad when he gets home," her mom replied.

❧

Gavin deposited his shoes in the closet and put his socks in the clothes hamper. As he undressed for bed, he grinned as he recalled his wife's wisdom. Instead of telling Holly she had to come home for the summer, Brianne had been right to let her come to her own decision.

Neither of them had expected the answer would be helping Meme with Papa.

He'd spoken to Parker about Blake staying in his NYC apartment for a couple of months in the summer. Parker said he'd have to see who else he'd scheduled to be there for that time period. Neither man was certain it was a good idea.

"It would test Blake's reliability," Parker admitted. "See if he's a stand-up guy. Who knows, we might even get to share our faith with him. I'm scheduled for at least one week in the apartment during the summer. I'd have to pray about it."

Gavin also had another reservation. It was the problem of letting his little girl go to the big city of Miami with only a frail elderly couple to look after her. Much to think about. Much to pray about.

31

Blake wasn't happy to hear that Holly might be spending part of her summer in Miami. Or that her dad might not allow her to spend a weekend in the Big Apple. "Why are your parents so protective," he whined. "I'm a good guy. Just ask my parents."

"Yeah. An objective source." Holly paused her reply. "I don't think my parents are being overly-protective. They don't want me to be serious about a guy when I'm only nineteen years old. They think a little separation might be good for us."

"Now you're talking like a grownup," he replied in a half-serious tone. "I can see their point. After all, as a lawyer I've got to consider both sides of a case. I guess I can date other girls and go out partying every weekend."

"Probably not if you're staying at my uncle's apartment," she chided. "He's probably got cameras everywhere."

"Always a hitch in my plans."

"Besides, Dad says interns often have to work on weekends, usually doing scut work no self-respecting lawyer would mess with."

"Maybe the lawyers in Miami are more compassionate." Holly hoped Blake was teasing. Surely, he wouldn't follow her to Miami. She felt like fly-paper again.

Friday night the family gathered around the dinner table for their last meal together before Holly flew back to DC for the last few weeks of school. She'd be home in time to see Ty graduate from high school.

Holly asked what Ty's plans were for the summer.

"About that," her dad jumped in. "We had a conversation with Ty this morning, and he's thinking about a different option."

Her mother spoke up. "Ty, are you still open to the idea?"

"What idea?" Holly could never wait patiently for the unknown.

"I am," Ty replied calmly. "And if we could keep Holly squirming about it until at least in the morning, I'm willing to save the discussion for later."

Holly looked for something to throw at her brother. Finding nothing suitable—or at least that wouldn't get her dismissed from the table—she pouted in silence.

Her lawyer father presented his case. "First, Nana may find suitable help for Meme by the time she returns from Florida. Thus, you, Holly, won't need to go at all." Holly nodded that she understood. "If Nana doesn't find help, your mother and I agree that sending you to Miami alone wouldn't be a good idea."

Holly turned shocked eyes on both of them. "I can take care of myself. I haven't been mugged in DC have I?"

He waved away her objection. "No, but you've also lived on campus. But that's not really the point. Papa won't want his great-granddaughter helping him to the restroom or dressing him. He'd be much more comfortable with Ty helping him. Not to mention that Ty is eight inches taller than you and about 60 pounds heavier."

Holly's lips parted in surprise and then returned to a pout. "So, you're sending Ty instead of me?"

Her mother spoke up. "Actually, we're thinking of sending both of you. While Ty helps Papa, you can help Meme with housework, cooking, and laundry." She winked at Holly. "When you learn how."

The siblings looked at each other. Ty offered a challenge. "Can you learn to be a team player, big sis? No bullying? No telling me what to do?"

Holly's defenses spiraled upward. Then, she pictured her sweet Meme's face and Papa's slow grin. She would do whatever was needed to please them both. She turned to Ty. "I'll be the best big sis you never had!" she teased. "We'll be the poster children for teamwork when these weeks are over."

Their parents gave each other looks of encouragement. Her mom summarized the situation. "All of our plans have to be tentative. First, Nana has to assess the situation. Then, if your help is needed, we'll send you to help out. Meanwhile, we'll all be doing what we can to find the Dyers help in Miami."

Everyone nodded agreement. They held hands around the table as Gavin said the blessing. "Lord, You know the plans You have for each of us. Give us Your wisdom as we seek Your guidance. And thank You for two special kids whose hearts have been touched by someone else's needs. Compassion is one of Your best gifts to us."

When Holly's semester ended, she waited the few days for Blake's commencement ceremony. His parents were flying from Los Angeles to see him graduate. Holly was eager to meet them. Blake had put her on the phone to them a few times during the year. She knew very little about them. What they had in common appeared to be their son.

Roland Chandler was an accountant and his wife, Carla, served as receptionist at a doctor's office in Long Beach. They were third generation Californians and lived in a cottage within walking distance of the ocean. It had also been in the family for some time. Holly could only imagine what it might be worth in its location if they sold it.

Blake made sure Holly was along to meet them at the airport when they landed. Both seemed very tired. They'd taken the red eye flight across the continent. They were in traveling clothes and looked good considering their long ordeal. Roland and Blake were about the same height but Roland seemed bigger—at least in girth. His hair and eyes were darker than Blake's. One look at Carla and Holly knew Blake's sandy hair and green eyes came from her gene pool. Carla was attractive and pleasant. Roland seemed a bit more intimidating.

His parents begged to go directly to their hotel, take a short nap, get cleaned up, and then, and only then, did they want a nice dinner. The Chandlers talked all the way to their hotel. Holly had nothing to add. She tried to squeeze in a question here and there, but Blake would cut her off with one of his exaggerated tales of campus life.

When Blake returned her to her dorm room, she collapsed on her single bed. In her family she was the storyteller extraordinaire. Now she was just the tag-along girlfriend.

32

By the time Holly had packed up her things from the dorm to ship home, stuffed clothes and personal items into her car, and left the capital city, she felt the familiar contrast of excitement and trepidation.

What would the summer hold for her? The next few weeks were planned but what would she do with the rest of her break? Uncle Parker had offered her tasks to do at the Nashville headquarters of the Sloan Foundation, including an easy role for Holly of being the office receptionist. She would enjoy that, but, once again, she longed to explore other fields of interest. Unfortunately, none came to mind. Her thoughts returned to the immediate future.

Nana's visit had done a world of good for Meme. Before she left Miami, Nana had lined up a caregiver. However, the person didn't work out as well as anticipated. Meme felt she had to supervise everything the woman did because she took no initiative in doing her tasks. She seemed to have little capacity for anticipating her patient's needs. As a result, Meme didn't feel free to leave her in charge while she ran errands or attempted to teach her Spanish Bible study class.

Would Ty and she be a better fit? They were scheduled to fly to Miami the day after her brother's graduation from Meadville High. They planned to stay for several weeks, or until Meme screamed into Nana's phone, "I can't stand the commotion one more minute."

Holly had promised always to use her inside voice. They both pledged not to argue in front of the grandparents. Holly wouldn't boss Ty, and Ty would do whatever Papa Phil needed—no matter how unpleasant. Since

Papa loved music, Ty would take his guitar and fill some of his great-grandpa's lonely moments. Holly knew she could spend hours listening to Meme's stories and hopefully soaking up some of her wisdom.

The trip home to Nashville from DC offered Holly a chance to think and pray. But the drive was physically exhausting. Practically every family member had offered to fly to DC and help her drive home. As she looked at the cluttered front passenger seat, she wondered where she would have put one of them. Besides, her stubborn, independent streak needed to prove that she could make the trip alone. Of course, she had to phone home every two hours, although her parents could track her movements on their cell phones. She was also warned that if she got home sooner than expected, her driving privileges would be suspended for a week.

With her car on the speed limit cruise control, the radio alternating with her playlist, frequent stops, and an overnight stay in Bristol, Tennessee, she reached home on the second day not a minute too early. She fell into a heap on her bed and dared anyone to make her get up for any reason. When she woke, the room had darkened. Her tummy rumbled. After a quick shower and change of clothes, she ambled into the kitchen looking for the plate of food her mom would have left for her after dinner.

Sure enough, she found a covered plate in the refrigerator. She placed it in the microwave, grabbed a glass of tea, and carried them into the family room. Her parents were curled on the couch watching an old black-and-white Alfred Hitchcock movie. Her dad pushed pause. "Where's Ty," she asked.

Her mom lifted her head off a throw pillow. "Practicing for graduation tomorrow. Wait 'til you see him in his maroon gown. Pretty handsome."

Her dad added, "Congratulations on a safe drive home. I'll help you unload your car while there's still some daylight left."

Her mom nodded to her husband, "And I'll tell you how the movie ends." He gave her a playful jab. "I'm pretty sure I know how it ends. You can tell me if I'm right." With his record of foretelling movie endings, both women were sure he would be. Holly wolfed the rest of her meal and went to her car to help her dad unload it. Once in her room, she'd start the tedious part of deciding what to put aside and what she'd need for her trip to Miami.

Ty's graduation went off without a hitch. One of their U.S. senators gave an inspiring talk about the virtues of service, whether it be in the military, local government, or their favorite nonprofit. Holly, who tended to think of her own needs first, felt inspired by his personal anecdotes and the stories of others who sacrificed for worthy causes.

After pictures, Ty headed to the lake with friends to water ski. Holly spent the rest of the day unpacking, packing, and repacking for her stay in Miami. When her phone rang, she took Hannah's call, relieved that it wasn't Blake on the line.

"Hello, girlfriend," Hannah began. "I assume you had an uneventful trip home, or I'm sure I would have heard about it."

"I did. Thank you for being on call if something had come up. Too bad I didn't need you to pull my car out of a ditch or change a tire."

"Oh, I wouldn't have done anything," she teased, "but listen with compassion. What are your plans for the evening?"

"You can come watch me pack," Holly volunteered.

"No way. You change your mind so much it takes forever. Instead, I'm putting you on the clock. Be through by four this afternoon, and I'll pick you up for a trip to get a smoothie. I barely remember what you look like."

"Will Seth be along for the ride?"

"Funny you should ask." Her sarcasm wasn't lost on Holly. "Seth left a week ago to be a summer camp counselor at a church conference center in Kentucky. So sorry you missed him."

"Me too. From what you've told me, I would have tried to steal him away from you."

"Not a chance. He detests short attractive brunettes with brown eyes and lively imaginations. See you at four."

When they clicked off, Holly decided to surprise everyone, including herself, by making quick decisions about her wardrobe in order to meet Hannah's deadline. With five minutes to spare, she'd fastened the luggage that would be checked at the airport, laid out her traveling clothes, and set her carry-on on her bathroom counter for all her makeup and hair products. She hurried to the front porch so Hannah might think she'd been sitting on the top step for ages.

After dinner Meme called Brianne to make sure everything was going as planned for the children's trip to Miami. "I can't wait for them to get here," she exclaimed. "I haven't seen them since Christmas."

Brianne assured her everything had been taken care of. Meme apologized that they would have to take an Uber from the airport to her house. "I just can't leave Papa alone. Yesterday was the caregiver's last day, praise God. I almost feel like today has been a holiday with her gone."

"I'm so sorry that didn't work out. Nana is using a different agency now to find a worthy replacement."

"For now, I'm thrilled to have my great-grands. Papa is eager to hear Ty play his guitar. We're going to have such a good time."

"I know you are," Brianne acknowledged, "but I'll miss my kids. Promise you'll tell me when you've had enough of their shenanigans."

"I'm sure God's up to something in this visit. You just wait and see."

33

The first few days in Miami were similar to a family reunion. Papa felt revitalized by the company. Although he sat in his favorite recliner most of the day, he loved hearing the great-grands talk and laugh and poke fun at each other. Meme's face glowed the entire time. He felt his dear wife needed the break from their confinement as much as he did.

When Ty pulled his guitar from its case, Papa felt heaven had come down. Meme found an old church hymnal, and Ty picked out the tunes to some of their favorites. Many of the songs he hadn't heard in years. The older couple sang some of the familiar tunes together in Spanish. That's how they had sung them in Ecuador. Papa missed the hymns since their present congregation sang more contemporary Christian music.

Imagine his surprise when Ty played a song he had written! Ty had a pleasant voice. All he needed was confidence in his ability. Papa piled on words of encouragement. The shy young man accepted the compliments—in the words of one of the hymns—as showers of blessings. Of course, his outgoing great-granddaughter liked the spotlight too. Could he detect a little jealousy at her lack of musical talent?

Nonetheless, she regaled them with tales from her drive from DC to Nashville. Holly was a born storyteller and added details Papa felt sure were mainly from her vivid imagination. She was funny too. He hadn't laughed so hard since she'd entertained her captive audience during their Christmas visit with Nana and Grandpa.

Papa still needed care. At first, he was uncomfortable with Ty's assistance with personal tasks. However, Ty had been tutored by his mother, who had needed care in many ways herself. He was feeling more comfortable asking for whatever his needs were. Ty was intuitive and quick to pick up on his signals. Papa thanked God repeatedly that this precious time with his great-grandson would leave lasting memories and spiritual blessings. Showers of them.

Meme couldn't believe her good fortune in having Holly's help. The young woman might not be as proficient at household tasks as she would have liked, but she was a determined learner. So what if her meringue flopped or she left clothes in the dryer until they wrinkled. These were easy fixes. In fact, she was reminded of her years of training her daughter Amy in similar ways.

When Amy was Holly's age, Meme had not become a Christian. The fortyish Jan Dyer had been a dutiful teacher to her young daughter, but she'd been a perfectionist, always demanding more of her offspring. She'd straightened her collars, pressed her clothes, and taught her impeccable table manners without ever giving her a strong sense of self. Meme scolded herself for being too busy making Amy over into her own image.

Neighbors had introduced the Dyers to Jesus through patient and subtle witnessing. At first, Amy was put off by her parents' love affair with Jesus. Although both she and Layton could see the changes Christ had already made in their walk with Him, they were skeptical that perhaps the Dyers had fallen into a cult. Even more amazing was the older couple's decision to volunteer for a short-term mission assignment in Ecuador.

Only when Brianne was diagnosed with her first bout of cancer at age four did Amy begin to look for a beam of hope. She began a relationship with Layton's pastor's wife, Myra Norwell, who was also battling cancer. Myra and Pastor Frank led Amy to the source of all hope, and she became a believer by trusting Christ as Savior.

Meme radically changed from giving Amy advice to offering encouragement, even under the most threatening circumstances of Brianne's illness. Thus, the phrase was born that would always define Meme: "God's up to something in this family. You just wait and see!"

✌

Holly and Ty sat in comfy wicker chairs on the Dyer's front porch. The pale moon shown on the quiet residential neighborhood, where most every house was dark. "It's too early to go to bed," Holly grumbled. "I haven't been asleep at this hour since I was eight."

Ty turned to face her. "Personally, I love the quiet. Even the neighbors' dogs have settled down for the night. I could sit here with my own thoughts until dawn. Don't you ever have a need for introspection?"

Holly gave the idea serious consideration. She finally muttered, "Not this way. I think as I'm doing something else. I think in the shower and as I drive. I don't remember ever thinking while sitting still."

"That's because you never sit still. Try it sometime." Holly turned her head and gave him a look he was quite familiar with. She resumed their conversation.

"I also think by talking. Don't you ever want to share what you're thinking with someone else—even if you're still thinking it?"

"I try to wait until my half-baked thoughts are more fully baked."

Holly couldn't resist a laugh. "I guess I bake them by talking. You may have a point. Have you baked any thoughts about our great-grands since you've been here?"

"Mom and Dad were right to send both of us. At first, I resisted taking care of an elderly man, even if he is my great-grandfather. I've already learned a lot from him: grace in the face of adversity. He doesn't complain. He's not bitter about his limitations. He manages his pain by focusing on me, us, his wife, anyone who crosses his path. I've never met anyone who shows more courage. I think that's where Mom gets it. Cancer doesn't change her focus."

Both sat silently, digesting the truth of Ty's words. Holly sat up in her chair. "Ty, Uncle Parker gave you a trophy for courage, remember?"

Ty looked dazed as though trying to remember Holly's reference. "He did?"

"Yes. You're in his trophy case of grace. He said you had courage in your actions but also courage in finding your true self." Ty's face broke into a huge grin. Holly continued, "Looks like Papa and Mom's character trait has passed to the next generation."

34

Holly and Meme stood at the kitchen counter washing and drying breakfast dishes. "Why don't you get a dishwasher Meme?" Holly picked up another plate to dry.

Meme looked around her kitchen. "When you've cooked over an open fire and washed dishes in a flowing creek, you think of a dishwasher as an extravagance. Besides, with just Papa and me eating here most of the time, we don't use enough dishes to fill up a dishwasher. Or if we waited until the dishwasher was full, we'd run out of dishes."

Holly grinned. "Maybe I should buy you some more dishes."

"Sweetie, I'm so blessed to have everything I need for the time I have left on this earth. In heaven, I'm sure I'll have a French chef and a banquet feast every day." Holly knew Meme was teasing, but her words left an imprint. How many girls her age had so many clothes that they couldn't decide what to take on a trip or leave behind?

Holly wiped the last dish and stacked it with the others. "You know what I love about you?" she asked. Meme shook her head no, although the beam in her eye indicated she was waiting for one of her great-granddaughter's gems. "Your perspective on things. I wish I could see material things in the same light as you do. I have so much—maybe too much—and yet I'm rarely satisfied. Why is that?"

"God will sort it out for you. It may come through a prayer to know Him better and love Him more. He's your source of contentment. Just ask St. Paul." Meme picked up her Bible, which was never far away, and turned to Philippians 4:11-13. She read aloud:

A Glimpse of Mercy

I am not saying this because I am in need, for I have
learned to be content whatever the circumstances. I know
what it is to be in need,
and I know what it is to have plenty. I have learned the
secret of being
content in any and every situation, whether well fed or
hungry, whether
living in plenty or in want. I can do all this through him
who gives me strength.

Holly walked to where Meme stood and embraced her. The two stood
in that pose for several minutes before Holly turned to face her. "Maybe
Ty is right. I can think while standing still." Meme's puzzled face told her
she had no idea what Holly was talking about. "I've got to go find Ty," she
muttered and then planted a kiss on Meme's cheek.

Ty was nervous. He'd never been in a Spanish-speaking group for Bible
study. Meme had insisted that he come along to her class while Holly cared
for Papa. The young adults greeted her as though she'd come from the Lost
Continent. Obviously, both students and teacher had missed each other
greatly after Papa became unable to attend with her.

Ty could keep up with the conversational flow. He was less sure of
using the Spanish language Bible he had been handed. After a lengthy time
of prayer requests and prayers, Meme explained why her great-grandson
was with her. Then she turned to Ty and asked him to share his Christian
testimony with the group.

Ty panicked. Then he remembered his pledge to be more open about
his faith. In fact, he'd practiced sharing a short account of his conversion
with Guillermo, whose family was very religious. But that had been months
ago. Awkwardly, he began with the events that led to his accepting Christ.
Since Meme had been an active part of his family since his birth, she was
able to fill in a word or a phrase when Ty got stuck.

As though the Holy Spirit took over, Ty shared about losing his way for
a time, feeling inadequate, doubting his own ability to make a difference

151

in the world. How his family and their former pastor had helped him to value the person God had made in His own image.

Then he picked up his guitar and began playing a song Meme had taught him in Spanish. The others joined in. Meme's Bible lesson followed from 1 John 5:10-13. She read the verses:

> He who has the Son has life; he who does not have the Son of God does not have life. I write these things to you who believe in the name of the Son of God so that you may know that you have eternal life. This is the confidence we have in approaching God.

After the worship service Ty drove Meme home. He waited for her to say something about why she had put him on the spot like that. When he finally got the nerve to ask her, she explained that most of her class had been exposed to many teachings about how to become a Christian. Many of them believed good works would save them. Others thought it was belonging to the right church. Some had grown up in spiritualism. She wanted Ty to share how he had come to know how belief in Jesus was the only way to know the one true God. She pulled out her ever-ready Bible and read him 1 Peter 3:15-16: *Always be prepared to give an answer to everyone who asks you to give the reason for the hope that you have.*

She closed the book and smiled the rest of the way home. Ty silently promised to practice giving his testimony in English as well as Spanish. Only the Lord knew when Meme might call on him again.

The great-grands had been in Florida for three weeks. Ty had guided Papa to one of the wicker chairs on the porch so they could enjoy the sights and sounds of children playing up and down the street. Meme and Holly were working in her flower beds in the cool of the early evening.

The experience was new to Holly, who kept grousing about her knees hurting. When a thorn from a rose bush pierced her thumb, she screamed in pain. Meme paid her no attention. A pretty garden was worth a few physical sacrifices. Holly carried on as though she'd have to call emergency services.

Just then Meme's cell rang. "Hello, Amy dear. ... No, Holly's fine. We're playing in the flower beds out front. You'd think she'd never seen dirt before. ... Okay, I'll put your call on speaker. Let me get up to the porch where Papa and Ty are sitting.

Meme rose from her knees and carried the phone to the porch. Holly joined her there, still sucking her thumb. Nana said hello to her grandchildren and father and shared her news. "I've finally found a home health aide who can come three days a week to help you with your needs. I'm working with a different agency. The aide's references are superb. In fact, she lives in a Miami suburb and would love to be that near her home. She's been staying round-the-clock with an elderly gentleman who has passed on." Nana let her words sink in.

"Her name is Amanda. The agency said she's asked for a week off." Nana gave them her starting date and asked Meme to tell her which three days she preferred.

Instead, Meme responded, "Who's paying for this?"

Nana hesitated. "Several people who love you very much. Don't worry about a thing."

Meme swallowed back tears. "We're very grateful, dear."

Papa took the phone from her and asked, "Is she pretty?" Everyone laughed as Meme jerked the phone away.

Holly and Ty looked at each other. They should have been happy to hear they would be flying home. Somehow, the week ahead seemed more like a long goodbye.

35

The two siblings stayed around to meet Amanda before flying home. Ty knew Holly would be able to give her parents a detailed description and assessment of the new aide. He just watched from a distance as Meme and Papa asked and answered questions. All he saw was a pleasant woman in her 50s with a round face and ready smile. She looked capable of helping Papa get up from bed and guide his walking. That's what he cared about most.

As they flew home side-by-side on the plane, they debriefed their experience in Miami. Holly told him she'd enjoyed learning household chores from Meme while hearing life lessons in the process. She regretted that staying with Papa meant not getting to go to church with Meme and meeting some of her friends. "But with your Spanish, you were much more help to her."

"I enjoyed being part of her Bible study class. I even made a few friends. A couple of the guys promised to text me. I hope they do. However, I didn't like Papa's suffering. He tried to hide it, but when he thought no one was looking, I'd sense him stiffen and see the pain in the set of his jaw. Maybe I should go into medicine and find a cure for his terrible disease."

Holly couldn't resist her pun. "You'd be the fastest doctor on the hall."

Ty took her humor in stride. "I could hurdle over the laundry baskets and high jump meal carts. See, here comes the stewardess down the aisle with the snack tray. I could practice now." He pretended to unfasten his seat belt as Holly fought to keep him in his strap.

"Meme said God was up to something in our visit. What do you think she meant?"

In his usual thoughtful way, Ty pursed his lips and considered his reply. "I definitely learned to be ready to share my faith." He grinned and continued. "Also, I think I'll feel more compassion for Mom and all she's been through with her cancer and treatments and replacing prostheses. I've been more concerned with how her pain affected me. I know I'll appreciate how she cares for our family without a word of complaint. Hey, it's not all about me you know." He readied himself for Holly's verbal jab.

Instead, she replied, "It's not all about me, either. I learned that I'm way too much into stuff. Fashion, shoes, purses, and did I mention shoes?" She looked down. "I need to clean out my closet and give a bunch of stuff to our church's clothes closet. Maybe I'll have some time before the next semester starts to volunteer at the food bank. The people in Meme's neighborhood barely survive paycheck to paycheck.

Ty looked at his sister with a hint of admiration.

After gleeful hugs at the airport and dinner at a Cracker Barrel Restaurant, the family arrived home. The kids headed to their rooms to unpack while Gavin and Brianne settled at the kitchen table to call their grandparents.

When Nana answered, she put the phone on speaker so Grandpa could hear the report. Brianne began the recounting with her children's impressions of Amanda. She went on to share some of their observations and potential concerns.

Gavin spoke up. "That's hearsay testimony since the witnesses aren't in the room. However, I'll let it stand for now." He pretended to gavel the table.

Nana laughed at the courtroom joke. "Meme says she's glad Amanda won't be staying overnight with them. She only lives fifteen minutes away and says she can be called at any hour of the day or night."

Brianne answered, "I'm sure your mother is glad about not cleaning up after my children any more. Her home will once again be peaceful."

"Oh, no," Nana objected. "Both of them talked about how much they enjoyed their visit with their great-grands. It was the first time they had been to the Dyer's home. The visit really perked up Papa and Meme, which, after all, was the primary purpose of the trip."

Nana paused. "Dad's doctor says his disease is progressing. We've got to be realistic about how long Mother can keep him at home."

Hannah was delighted when Holly told her she'd decided to spend the remaining weeks of the summer at home. "What about Blake and trips to New York City?" she'd asked.

"He's resigned to his fate. He's had a rough time with the long hours at the law office, finding a roommate, and moving into a small apartment that he and Keith might live in while they attend Columbia Law School. He said Dad was right about him having to pick up work on the weekends. I don't see how we could have worked in a visit anyhow."

Holly reported that his calls had been infrequent, and he always sounded stressed.

Hannah was delighted to have Holly back in the college class at church. She'd raised her eyebrows and gasped when Holly shared with the class that she was giving away clothes, shoes, and accessories to the church clothes closet and volunteering at the food pantry. "And Parker arranged for me to work in the office at the medical clinic he once served as director. I'm so busy filing medical records I sometimes forget I'm on vacation." Everyone laughed.

Hannah liked seeing a more mature and thoughtful version of Holly, the social butterfly and carefree teenager who'd lived in a privileged cocoon. *She's growing up,* Hannah mused as she listened to her friend share some of Meme's wisdom with her. One of the memories was what Meme had taught her about contentment.

"God's work on earth doesn't get done by thinking about it," Meme had said. "Every moment counts as an opportunity to give God glory. But He smiles when we rest, just as He did on the seventh day of creation. Enjoy God's rest, my dear. Having to do something all the time is denying Him a blessing." Then she'd opened her Bible to the Book of Hebrews and read, *There remains, then, a Sabbath-rest for the people of God; ... Let us, therefore, make every effort to enter that rest* (Hebrews 4:9, 10).

Wow, thought Hannah. Holly was always on the go. She'd be interested to see if her friend's great-grandmother's words would make a difference in how Holly handled the pace of her life.

36

Ty reported to Middle Tennessee State University for fall training. As a track scholarship recipient, he lived in one of the athletic dorms. The rooms reminded him of movies about military barracks: sparse furniture, a roommate he'd never met, and duty call early each morning. The difference seemed to be that the coaches didn't care if or how he made his bed.

The food was to die for. Ty had been reared on healthy options, so the veggies were nothing new. Some of the guys gripped about the absence of their favorite southern dishes, deep-fried or smothered in gravies. As opposed to the Hamilton house, the cafeteria staff allowed them to eat all they wanted. Ty soon found out why as he collapsed on his bunk one evening after his first week there. So far, he'd lost five pounds. He liked the coach, the routine, the variety of track and field options he'd been exposed to. Most of the time was taken up in conditioning and endurance training.

His roommate went by the name of Mort. Ty guessed he would too if his name were Morton. Mort was from a small town in Western Tennessee. He hadn't competed in the same division as Meadville High, so Ty had never met him at competitions. Mort was a high-jumper. They usually only saw each other at night or occasionally at meals. Ty wanted to feel him out on spiritual things. The first Sunday Ty offered Mort a ride to church, but he'd opened one eye briefly when Ty tried to wake him.

Ty enjoyed the church experience so much that he decided to attend the college Bible study that night. Mort told him he had other plans, so Ty went alone. Mort hadn't returned to the room by the time Ty was ready to call it a night. He sat on the edge of his bed, hands clasped between his knees, and asked his Heavenly Father for guidance. "Lord, you've put Mort and me together for a reason. I don't want to presume to know why. Let our relationship develop on your timing. And if I get a chance to share my testimony, you know I'm ready."

Several nights later, Ty grabbed his guitar from its case. He felt a tune coming on. As his fingers strummed, words began to form. He hummed at first but then began to sing softly. It was the first time he'd picked up his guitar since moving into the dorm.

Guys came from all directions to find out where the live music was coming from. Ty was used to being teased about his songwriting, so he quickly switched to a more familiar country song. A couple of guys joined in while others garbled the lyrics and tried to steal the show.

As time went by, gathering in Ty's room for a jam session became a welcome relief from their exhausting days in the gym. One of the guys asked Ty if he knew a contemporary gospel song. Ty started playing, and a surprising number of guys joined in. Others filtered away.

Mort sat on his bed, phone in hand, absorbed in a video game.

Ty continued to meet with his Uncle Parker each month. Their August hamburger fest would be his last before classes started. They met on a Saturday shortly after the lunch crowd had dwindled to the point that they could hear themselves talk.

"What? No French fries?" Parker asked his nephew.

"I'm in training, remember?"

Parker changed his order to a side salad. "No way I'm going to let you out-muscle me."

Ty rolled his eyes. His uncle was the most buff man he'd ever met. When their orders arrived, Parker wanted to know all about the track team. Later, when Ty pushed his empty basket away, he looked intently at his uncle. "How do you get someone who's not interested in spiritual things to go to church with you?"

"You got someone specific in mind?"

"My roommate. He sleeps in every Sunday. Sometimes at night I play my guitar and a few of us guys sing. Lately, we've sung some spiritual songs. Mort just ignores us. In your book, the one you dedicated to me—"

"Yes, *Saved to Serve*," Parker interrupted. "What about it?"

"You told about how you weren't interested in going to chapel when you were in prison. But you finally did. A cellmate helped you want to go. What did he do? I'm just asking for a friend." Both guys chuckled.

"Ah, Malcolm, my dear cellie. Do you know he runs one of the Sloan halfway houses in Miami now?" Ty nodded. Parker crossed his hands in front of him on the table and grew serious. "First, you've got to pray for that person. Plead with God for his salvation. Second, you've got to be the real deal. Live your testimony. Maybe he'll notice and wonder what makes you different. Third, count on God's timing. You're a seed planter. God reaps the harvest. Fourth, keep giving the guy opportunities to turn you down. If he ever asked why you're so interested in his spiritual welfare, be ready to share your faith."

"I can even do that in Spanish," Ty announced. Parker raised his eyebrows. "Never mind," Ty explained. "That's another story. But thanks, Uncle Parker. What you said really makes sense. I know God has given me Mort as a roommate for a reason."

"I'll pray for Mort along with you." His uncle sat back in his seat and eyed his nephew. "You've sure grown in your faith these past few months. I'm proud of you."

Eight months ago, Ty would have thought he'd never hear those words from his uncle. He'd been too busy comparing himself to others and finding fault. Now the two headed for the door, Parker's arm around Ty shoulder as they talked their way to their vehicles.

37

Holly's departure for the fall semester of her sophomore year at Georgetown was full of all the drama, tears, and hugs required for such an occasion. When she arrived at the carousel to pick up her luggage at Reagan Airport, she spotted her new roommate for the semester. Although they had never met, they had exchanged texts and viewed each other's social media sites.

Leticia waved her outstretched arm at Holly and wound her way through the throng of people waiting for their bags. Holly grabbed her for a hug, always assuming everyone was a friend unless they proved otherwise. She was immediately taken with Leticia's smooth brown skin, eyes darker than Holly's, and hair that made Holly's brunette locks look pale in comparison.

"You're beautiful!" Holly exclaimed. Leticia looked surprised by the greeting. She'd soon learn that Holly's first impressions almost always were the first words out of her mouth.

The young women boarded the subway that would take them to the drop-off point for Georgetown University.

Amy Brooks wasn't at all pleased by what she was hearing from Miami. Amanda, the home health aide, wasn't the problem. She had worked out wonderfully. Her dad liked her immensely. They joked with each other so much that her mom often couldn't tell when either one was serious.

The problem was Papa's health, which seemed to decline inch-by-inch.

Despite new medicines and Amanda's thoughtful care, Papa Phil was less mobile and in increasing discomfort. Her mom fretted over him, although she admitted that worry doesn't accomplish anything. Recently, on the phone she'd reminded her daughter of Hebrews 9:27. "We are all destined to die. Every day is a gift of God. That's why they call it the present."

Amy had kept Brianne informed of her grandfather's condition. Both women decided that the great-grands didn't need to know every setback.

By October, Amy couldn't stand being so far away from her parents at such a difficult time. She and Layton flew to Miami for an indefinite stay to give her mom some respite. Only because Holly was coming home for Thanksgiving did they return to Nashville.

Days before Holly was due home, Amanda called early one morning. The call wasn't unexpected—just unwelcomed. Phil Dyer had passed peacefully in his sleep with his dear wife by his bedside. No arrangements had been made.

Layton held his wife in his arms as she wept—not so much for her dad, who was now pain-free and in the presence of His Lord—but for herself, her mom, and everyone who would feel his loss in the coming weeks, months, and years. Amy waited for her mother's call, knowing she had many details to attend to at present. That afternoon the call from Meme came through.

Years ago, after the Dyers had moved to Florida, they had agreed to be buried in a Nashville cemetery. That was the beginning of the family plot that had been purchased to include Layton and Amy when the time came.

When Holly arrived home, the Brooks and the Hamilton family flew to Miami. After a moving tribute to Phil at the funeral service, the Dyers' church held a reception for them in their fellowship hall. Then, the Spanish congregation celebrated Phil's passing in their heart language. Ty served as interpreter for his family. He was pleased to see several of the young people he had met the previous summer. Everyone had kind words for Señor Phil.

The Brooks, Meme Dyer, and the Hamiltons flew to Nashville with the body for a private service at the cemetery. There Parker and Kathy, Olivia Hamilton, Hannah and her family, and other church and business friends shared their own words of comfort with the grieving family. The surprise attendee appeared in a wheelchair bundled head to toe for the cool weather. Holly and Ty whispered at the same time, "Pastor Frank!" Layton steered his chair under the family tent. His pastor was, after all, used by God to bring this family together.

Gathered around the Hamilton dinner table that evening, a solemn family picked at the casseroles, salads, and desserts brought by their Nashville church family. Brianne seemed to be taking her grandfather's death the hardest. Layton sat beside his only child trying to think of something helpful to say. Then a past memory came to mind.

"Brianne, do you remember your Grandmother Brooks' funeral? You were just a little girl at the time."

"Maybe. A little bit. Wasn't my Uncle Kyle there?

"Yes. He was in the military at the time."

"What did you want me to remember from it?"

"At the dinner table that night, just like now, I got a lump in my throat. You spoke up, 'Daddy, you know Grandmother is in heaven. Don't cry.' Then, a few minutes later, Myra Norwell called. She too had been crying. Do you know what she said to me?"

"No. I do remember how sad I felt when Mrs. Norwell died of cancer."

"Myra said sorrow shared is divided in half. All of us"— Layton pointed at the others around the table — "are sharing each other's sorrow and lessening its weight."

Meme Dyer stayed with her daughter and son-in-law "at least through Christmas." After she returned to Miami, she had a long list of things to be done due to Phil's passing. Amy talked it over with Layton, and together they decided to ask Meme to consider moving in with them when she was ready.

Meme had already claimed a sofa chair beside a large end table in the living room. There she laid her glasses, devotional book and Bible, box of tissues, and a crystal dish full of small candies. One afternoon when the house was quiet, the couple approached her with the idea.

"Oh, pshaw!" she said. "I wouldn't want to be right here under foot for the rest of my life."

Layton grinned mischievously. "Oh, I wouldn't want you under my feet. They get awfully smelly after I've been to the gym."

Recovering the conversation, Amy chimed in. "We've been thinking. What if we turned Amy Interiors into a suite for you. Now that I'm semi-retired, I don't need that warehouse space or even that office. It would make a lovely sitting area, bedroom, and bath. You'd have plenty of privacy at the back of the house. I've already got ideas swirling in my head."

Meme quickly responded, "I'll bet you do. I can see the wheels turning." She paused. "Let the idea simmer. For now, I want to be with Phil's things, his rocking chair, his mementoes. I need to be near him." Her face crumbled as tears began to weave their way down her cheeks. Amy rushed her a tissue.

"The idea is officially on simmer," Layton said.

Ty enjoyed living close to his grandparents. Murfreesboro was a short trip east on I-24. Since track season was still a few months away, he often dropped by to visit. He also enjoyed having Meme to himself. One afternoon he stopped by on his way to play an opening set for another musician at a night spot on Broadway.

Layton had gone to the gym, and Amy was staging a residence for an open house. Meme made him some herbal tea—not his favorite beverage—but he accepted it graciously. Settling back into the sofa, cup in hand, he told her, "Meme, I think I've found my true love."

Meme set her cup on the end table and clapped her hands excitedly. "Oh, you're such a handsome young man. I knew the lord would lead you to some lovely lady soon. Tell me about her."

"It—it's not a young lady." Meme eyebrows shot together. "It's music. Music is my heart language. I run the track playing songs in my head, lyrics coming out of nowhere. After this next semester, I'm thinking of changing my major."

"Have you told your parents?" she asked.

"No. I'm telling you. It's just between us for now."

Meme got a quirky smile on her face. "Then I think we ought to let it simmer."

Brooks-Hamilton

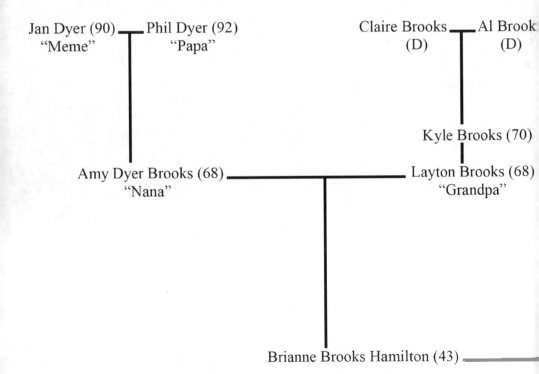

Jan Dyer (90) —— Phil Dyer (92)
"Meme"   "Papa"

Claire Brooks —— Al Brook
      (D)   (D)

Kyle Brooks (70)

Amy Dyer Brooks (68) ————————————— Layton Brooks (68)
       "Nana"   "Grandpa"

Brianne Brooks Hamilton (43)

Family Tree*

*Listed by age in 2018
(D) = Deceased

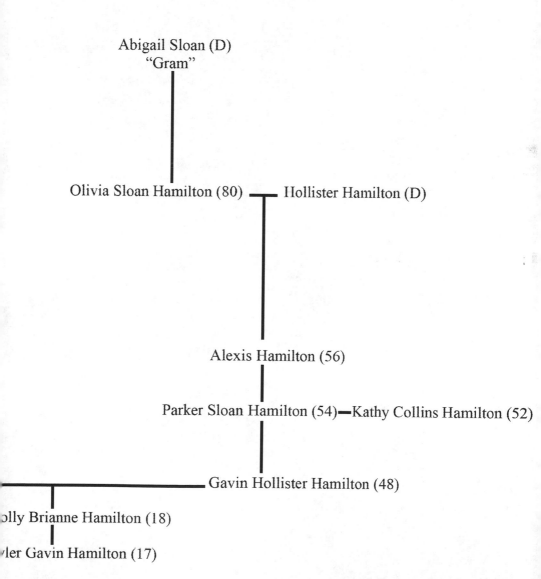

Abigail Sloan (D)
"Gram"

Olivia Sloan Hamilton (80) —— Hollister Hamilton (D)

Alexis Hamilton (56)

Parker Sloan Hamilton (54)—Kathy Collins Hamilton (52)

Gavin Hollister Hamilton (48)

olly Brianne Hamilton (18)

·ler Gavin Hamilton (17)

READER'S GUIDE

Use these questions for personal reflection or group study:

1. How did the book receive its name, *A Glimpse of Mercy?* Give an example of a character who extended mercy? Received mercy?
2. Explain Holly's discomfort around the phone calls from her boyfriend Blake?
3. What did Ty feel he had to prove to his family?
4. How did each family member react to Brianne's latest cancer diagnosis?
5. Explain how Parker helped Ty overcome his self-image problems?
6. How was Grandmother Olivia's illness the key to unlocking her heart?
7. How did Olivia come to know Jesus as Savior?
8. Why are Holly and Hannah such good friends for each other?
9. What did Holly and Ty learn from their trip to stay with their great-grandparents?
10. What did Ty discover is his true love?
11. Who is your favorite character in this book? Why?
12. Define mercy. Tell about a time you were shown mercy; showed mercy to someone else.
13. Who received a trophy to go in Layton Brooks's trophy case?

MEET THE AUTHOR

BETTY J HASSLER combines her gift of writing with seventeen years of experience in Christian publishing and forty years as a minister's wife. Her true-to-life stories illustrate how families can grow in their faith despite life's difficult twists and turns.

Dr. Hassler is an accomplished writer of numerous magazine articles, study guides, workbooks, and interactive learning activities. She has co-written books, edited books for publication, and served as editor of two magazines with a combined readership of more than 750,000. This is her third novel in the Trophies of Grace series.

A native Texan, she received graduate and post-graduate degrees from Baylor University and Southwestern Baptist Theological Seminary. She has led conferences, Bible studies, and discipleship groups in addition to being a keynote speaker and serving on panel discussions.

Dr. Hassler is married, the mother of two, and a grandmother. Her family lives near Pensacola, Florida, where she enjoys her book clubs, mentoring, and church activities.

TO FIND OUT MORE ABOUT BETTY J HASSLER AND HER NOVELS, VISIT HER WEBSITE AT *www.bettyjhassler.com*.

Coming Soon
The fourth and final novel in the
Trophies of Grace series
Book 4

A Taste *of* Joy

Turn the page for a preview of Chapter 1.

Holly Brianne Hamilton sat on a rocky beach in southern California. Sand covered her wet suit. In fact, her face, hands, and feet felt gritty to the touch. She watched the beachcombers up and down the coast on a Thursday afternoon. "How do these people stand the blowing wind?" she asked to no one in particular.

Billowy clouds separated the ocean from the December sky. In the distance, she picked out Blake's surfboard riding a high wave toward shore. She ran her fingers through her long, tangled hair as he carried his board up the hillside toward her. His patterned wet suit matched his surfboard, which she supposed was meant to impress her. She had to admit the effect was picture perfect.

That's the problem, Lord. Holly easily lapsed into conversations with Jesus, and this one had her nose wrinkled and her lips in a downward spiral. *Is this relationship mostly about external stuff? Is it ever going to be about You, Blake, and me in the same sentence?*

In her heart of hearts, Holly knew Blake probably wasn't—maybe, couldn't be—God's choice for her forever partner. Yet, he was so convinced he was. Sometimes she felt overpowered by his confidence, as though he spoke for both of them. Did she really have a mind of her own? Was it too easy to go along with him when he dreamed aloud about their life together?

She reflected on how Blake had been pursuing her since she was a freshman at Georgetown University in Washington, DC, where they were students. She'd tried many times to pull away, to date others, to have her independence. Blake would wait her out, appearing just often enough to keep him at the top of her mind, doing endearing things, and offering a listening ear. She simply didn't know how to say *no* to Blake Chandler's charm.

When she began dating Blake, Holly had told her best friend from high school, Hannah Harper, all about him. "What's not to like?" Hannah had asked. "Sandy hair and green eyes? Muscular California beach boy physique? Political science major? He interns at your Uncle Parker's nonprofit in DC. Must be a good guy."

Hannah had been right, of course. Nothing about Blake was hard to like. Except that one thing.

She recalled their first meeting at the lobbying firm of The Sloan Foundation, where they both worked. The Foundation supported numerous halfway houses for ex-cons, drug rehabilitation centers, and a lobbying effort on behalf of prison reform. Blake worked as a staff intern to earn credit for his political science major. Since Holly had practically grown up with The Sloan Foundation, their jobs were very different. However, Blake had quickly noticed her. Was it because she was the niece of the founder? He claimed it was her outgoing personality—and maybe a little about her very attractive appearance.

Now a graduate of Georgetown University and Columbia Law School, Blake had taken an entry-level job at a prestigious law firm in New York. He'd recently passed the bar exam and hoped to practice law in Washington, DC. Holly knew her graduation from Georgetown next May —conveniently in the same city—would present new challenges for their relationship. What then? Her business degree would prepare her for many opportunities but nothing too specialized.

Blake seemed to know the answer to the question of her future, but Holly didn't have the same assurance. That's why she was here. At Blake's home in Long Beach for the beginning of Christmas break. To have the talk.

Thursday evening Holly and Blake sat outside on his parents' porch bench sipping from mugs of hot tea. Holly gazed at the row of clapboard houses across the street. Blake certainly hadn't come from a moneyed family. His parents were the second generation to live here. With the beach a few blocks away, the modest ranch style three-bedroom home sat in a perfect location. It would sell for far more than it was worth; however, she guessed it would be in the family for years to come. An only child, Blake would want to keep his childhood home—plus the convenient access to the beach.

"You're quiet this evening," Blake observed. "Care to share what you're thinking?"

Not really, she mused. Tonight's the night. If she could just get her heart and her head in the same place, she was reasonably sure this feeling of dread would go away. But the two weren't even close.

Blake tried again. "Do I have to order a cat scan to see if there's brain activity in that gorgeous head of yours?" He ran his fingers through her long dark hair.

"You can't. You're a lawyer, not a doctor. But thanks for the compliment."

"Now that we've established contact between us, what's going on? The last time you were this quiet, you were sick with the flu."

Holly guessed he was right. She had a bit of a reputation as a drama queen. She could talk her way into and out of troublesome conversations. She glanced his way, smitten as usual by his handsome face, memories of him in his wet suit filling her mind with all the wrong images. Why couldn't she just break Blake's heart and be done with it? Tomorrow she would fly to Nashville to be with her family for the rest of her Christmas holiday.

She took a deep breath. "Blake, we've been together, on and off, for almost four years. I know you want to plan the next steps in our relationship, and you've been pretty clear as to what they should be."

"Hold on." He sat up straighter. "Until I get a job in DC, I don't have much to offer you. We can postpone this conversation for a few more months."

"No, we can't." Holly swallowed. "I need to be as clear with you as you have been with me. Honestly, I'm at a loss for words."

Blake grabbed an imaginary microphone. "Hear that, ladies and gentlemen. A first in the life of Holly Hamilton—"

She batted his hand away. "Seriously, I've got to explain my feelings. I've tried before—many times, in fact. So let me try again."

For the next half hour Holly talked and Blake listened. When she bowed her head and wept, she struggled to resist leaning on his shoulder for comfort. But from what she'd said tonight, that wouldn't be an appropriate response. *I just need time and space,* she told herself.

Back in Holly's hometown of Nashville, Tennessee, a drama unfolded at the home of her maternal grandparents, Layton and Amy Brooks. Her great-grandmother, Jan "Meme" Dyer, sat in her favorite chair in the Brooks' living room studying the crossword puzzle in front of her. Holly's grandmother, "Nana" Brooks, entered the living room and looked with exasperation at her mother. "Meme, you've got to go to bed. It's almost midnight."

"Do I have a curfew?" her mother groused. "Why can't you just go to *you*r bed?"

Mother was in a mood, Nana decided, very unlike the normally sweet woman who'd spent years ministering in Ecuador and then in Florida. In fact, it was so unlike her mother to be grouchy that Nana moved to her side and put a hand on her forehead.

Meme brushed it aside. Her daughter sat down on the sofa beside her chair, dust cloth in hand, and began wiping the polished oak coffee table. "I'd like to get this room picked up before we call it a night." She motioned toward the candy wrappers and soda can on the side table near Meme's favorite chair.

"Your house has never been messy in its entire life," the older woman contended. "It looks like something out of a *Southern Living* magazine and you know it. After all, you're a retired interior decorator and home stylist." Meme emphasized the word *retired*.

"Once upon a time," Nana sighed. "Now this place looks like a grandma's house. I'm afraid I haven't kept up with the latest styles."

"Oh, pooh, who cares? Here let me help with that." She took the dust cloth and began wiping the table. Meme definitely had a mind of her own, Nana observed. Even into her nineties, she liked her independence. She had moved in with her daughter and son-in-law after her husband Phil passed away.

Just then Grandpa Brooks, clad in warm pajamas, walked in and surveyed the scene. "Dusting at this hour? What's up?" Two sets of eyes stared him down.

Grandpa crossed his arms. "I think I'm detecting a bit of anxiety about what's going on with Holly about now. She's due back in town Friday night." He looked at his watch, which he still wore on his wrist. "California is a couple of hours behind Central Standard Time in Nashville. Let's see, it would be about ten o'clock Thursday on Holly's last night at Blake's house ... hum."

Neither woman contradicted him. Finally, his wife spoke up. "Well, I suppose she and her boyfriend are having 'the talk' about their future. Isn't that something to be anxious about?"

"Knowing Holly, we'll hear all about it soon enough. How about instead of cleaning"—he reached for the dust rag —"we pray." The threesome grabbed hands as Layton led a prayer for his granddaughter Holly and her boyfriend, Blake Chandler.

When he finished, Meme added, "Lord God, I know You have this well in hand. I just can't wait to see what You're up to."

04099286-00851086

Printed in the United States
by Baker & Taylor Publisher Services